URSULA K. LE GUIN

"Queen of the Realm of Fantasy"
—*Washington Post*

Winner of the Hugo and Nebula awards
The World Fantasy Award
The National Book award

"Like all great writers of fiction, Ursula K. Le Guin creates imaginary worlds that restore us, hearts eased, to our own." —*Boston Globe*

"Her characters are complex and haunting, and her writing is remarkable for its sinewy grace." —*Time*

"She wields her pen with a moral and psychological sophistication rarely seen. What she really does is write fables: splendidly intricate and hugely imaginative tales about such mundane concerns as life, death, love, and sex." —*Newsweek*

"Idiosyncratic and convincing, Le Guin's characters have a long afterlife." —*Publishers Weekly*

"Her worlds are haunting psychological visions molded with firm artistry" —*Library Journal*

"If you want excess and risk and intelligence, try Le Guin." —*San Francisco Chronicle*

T0152997

PM PRESS OUTSPOKEN AUTHORS SERIES

THE WILD GIRLS

plus...

THE WILD GIRLS

GIRLS

plus

"Staying Awake While We Read"

and

"A Lovely Art"
Outspoken Interview

URSULA K. LE GUIN

PM PRESS | 2011

"The Wild Girls" was first published in *Asimov's Science Fiction* magazine in March 2002. It has been revised by the author for this edition.
"Staying Awake While we Read" first appeared in *Harper's Magazine*, February 2008. This is its first book publication.
"The Conversation of the Modest" is published here for the first time.

Series Editor: Terry Bisson

ISBN: 978-1-60486-403-8
LCCN: 2010916472

PM Press
P.O. Box 23912
Oakland, CA 94623
PMPress.org

Cover: John Yates/Stealworks.com
Inside design: Josh MacPhee/Justseeds.org

CONTENTS

THE WILD GIRLS

BELA TEN BELEN WENT ON A FORAY with five companions. There had been no nomad camps near the City for several years, but harvesters in the Eastern Fields reported seeing smoke of fires beyond the Dayward Hills, and the six young men announced that they'd go see how many camps there were. They took with them as guide Bidh Handa, who had guided forays against the nomad tribes before. Bidh and his sister had been captured from a nomad village as children and grew up in the City as slaves. Bidh's sister Nata was famous for her beauty, and Bela's brother Alo had given her owner a good deal of the Belen family wealth to get her for his wife.

Bela and his companions walked and ran all day following the course of the East River up into the hills. In the evening they came to the crest of the hills and saw on the plains below them, among watermeadows and winding streams, three circles of the nomads' skin huts, strung out quite far apart.

"They came to the marshes to gather mudroots," the guide said. "They're not planning a raid on the Fields of the City. If they were, the three camps would be close together."

"Who gathers the roots?" Bela ten Belen asked.

"Men and women. Old people and children stay in the camps."

"When do the people go to the marshes?"

"Early in the morning."

"We'll go down to that nearest camp tomorrow after the gatherers are gone."

"It would be better to go to the second village, the one on the river," Bidh said.

Bela ten Belen turned to his soldiers and said, "Those are this man's people. We should shackle him."

They agreed, but none of them had brought shackles. Bela began to tear his cape into strips.

"Why do you want to tie me up, lord?" the Dirt man asked with his fist to his forehead to show respect. "Have I not guided you, and others before you, to the nomads? Am I not a man of the City? Is not my sister your brother's wife? Is not my nephew your nephew, and a god? Why would I run away from our City to those ignorant people who starve in the wilderness, eating mudroots and crawling things?" The Crown men did not answer the Dirt man. They tied his legs with the lengths of twisted cloth, pulling the knots in the silk so tight they could not be untied but only cut open. Bela appointed three men to keep watch in turn that night.

Tired from walking and running all day, the young man on watch before dawn fell asleep. Bidh put his legs into the coals of their fire and burned through the silken ropes and stole away.

When he woke in the morning and found the slave gone, Bela ten Belen's face grew heavy with anger, but he said only, "He'll have warned that nearest camp. We'll go to the farthest one, off there on the high ground."

"They'll see us crossing the marshes," said Dos ten Han.

"Not if we walk in the rivers," Bela ten Belen said.

And once they were out of the hills on the flat lands they walked along streambeds, hidden by the high reeds and willows that grew on the banks. It was autumn, before the rains, so the water was shallow enough that they could make their way along beside it or wade in it. Where the reeds grew thin and low and the stream widened out into the marshes, they crouched down and found what cover they could.

By midday they came near the farthest of the camps, which was on a low grassy rise like an island among the marshes. They could hear the voices of people gathering mudroot on the eastern side of the island. They crept up through the high grass and came to the camp from the south. No one was in the circle of skin huts but a few old men and women and a little swarm of children. The children were spreading out long yellow-brown roots on the grass, the old people cutting up the largest roots and putting them on racks over low fires to hasten the drying. The six Crown men came among them suddenly with their swords drawn. They cut the throats of the old men and women. Some children ran away down into the marshes. Others stood staring, uncomprehending.

Young men on their first foray, the soldiers had made no plans—Bela ten Belen had said to them, "I want to go out there and kill some thieves and bring home slaves," and that was all the plan they wanted. To his friend Dos ten Han he had said, "I want to get some new Dirt girls, there's not one in the City I can stand to look at." Dos ten Han knew he was thinking about the beautiful no-mad-born woman his brother had married. All the young Crown men thought about Nata Belenda and wished they had her or a girl as beautiful as her.

"Get the girls," Bela shouted to the others, and they all ran at the children, seizing one or another. The older children had mostly fled at once, it was the young ones who stood staring or began too late to run. Each soldier caught one or two and dragged them back to the center of the village where the old men and women lay in their blood in the sunlight.

Having no ropes to tie the children with, the men had to keep hold of them. One little girl fought so fiercely, biting and scratching, that the soldier dropped her, and she scrabbled away screaming shrilly for help. Bela ten Belen ran after her, took her by the hair, and cut her throat to silence her screaming. His sword was sharp and her neck was soft and thin; her body dropped away from her head, held on only by the bones at the back of the neck. He dropped the head and came running back to his men. "Take one you can carry and follow me," he shouted at them.

"Where? The people down there will be coming," they said. For the children who had escaped had run down to the marsh where their parents were.

"Follow the river back," Bela said, snatching up a girl of about five years old. He seized her wrists and slung her on his back as if she were a sack. The other men followed him, each with a child, two of them babies a year or two old.

The raid had occurred so quickly that they had a long lead on the nomads who came straggling up round the hill following the children who had run to them. The soldiers were able to get down into the rivercourse, where the banks and reeds hid them from people looking for them even from the top of the island.

The nomads scattered out through the reedbeds and meadows west of the island, looking to catch them on their way back to the City. But Bela had led them not west but down a branch of the river that led off southeast. They trotted and ran and walked as best they could in the water and mud and rocks of the riverbed. At first they heard voices far behind them. The heat and light of the sun filled the world. The air above the reeds was thick with stinging insects. Their eyes soon swelled almost closed with bites and burned with salt sweat. Crown men, unused to carrying burdens, they found the children heavy, even the little ones. They struggled to go fast but went slower and slower along the winding channels of the water, listening for the nomads behind them. When a child made any noise, the soldiers slapped or shook it till it was still. The girl Bela ten Belen carried hung like a stone on his back and never made any sound.

When at last the sun sank behind the Dayward Hills, that seemed strange to them, for they had always seen the sun rise behind those hills.

They were now a long way south and east of the hills. They had heard no sound of their pursuers for a long time. The gnats and mosquitoes growing even thicker with dusk drove them at last up onto a drier meadowland, where they could sink down in a place where deer had lain, hidden by the high grasses. There they all lay while the light died away. The great herons of the marsh flew over with heavy wings. Birds down in the reeds called. The men heard each other's breathing and the whine and buzz of insects. The smaller children made tiny whimpering noises, but not often, and not loud. Even the babies of the nomad tribes were used to fear and silence.

As soon as the soldiers had let go of them, making threatening gestures to them not to try to run away, the six children crawled together and huddled up into a little mound, holding one another. Their faces were swollen with insect bites and one of the babies looked dazed and feverish. There was no food, but none of the children complained.

The light sank away from the marshes, and the insects grew silent. Now and then a frog croaked, startling the men as they sat silent, listening.

Dos ten Han pointed northward: he had heard a sound, a rustling in the grasses, not far away.

They heard the sound again. They unsheathed their swords as silently as they could.

Where they were looking, kneeling, straining to see through the high grass without revealing themselves, suddenly a ball of faint light rose up and wavered in the air above the grasses, fading and brightening. They heard a voice, shrill and faint, singing. The hair stood up on their heads and arms as they stared at the bobbing blur of light and heard the meaningless words of the song.

The child that Bela had carried suddenly called out a word. The oldest, a thin girl of eight or so who had been a heavy burden to Dos ten Han, hissed at her and tried to make her be still, but the younger child called out again, and an answer came.

Singing, talking, and babbling shrilly, the voice came nearer. The marsh fire faded and burned again. The grasses rustled and shook so much that the men, gripping their swords, looked for a whole group of people, but only one head appeared among the grasses. A single child came walking towards them. She kept talking, stamping, waving her hands so that they would know she was not trying to surprise them. The soldiers stared at her, holding their heavy swords.

She looked to be nine or ten years old. She came closer, hesitating all the time but not stopping, watching the men all the time but talking to the children. Bela's girl got up and ran to her and they clung to each other. Then, still watching the men, the new girl sat down with the other children. She and Dos ten Han's girl talked a little in low voices. She held Bela's girl in her arms, on her lap, and the little girl fell asleep almost at once.

"It must be that one's sister," one of the men said.

"She must have tracked us from the beginning," said another.

"Why didn't she call the rest of her people?"

"Maybe she did."

"Maybe she was afraid to."

"Or they didn't hear."

"Or they did."

"What was that light?"

"Marsh fire."

"Maybe it's them."

They were all silent, listening, watching. It was almost dark. The lamps of the City of Heaven were being lighted, reflecting the lights of the City of Earth, making the soldiers think of that city, which seemed as far away as the one above them in the sky. The faint bobbing light had died away. There was no sound but the sigh of the night wind in the reeds and grasses.

The soldiers argued in low voices about how to keep the children from running off during the night. Each may have thought that he would be glad enough to wake and find them gone, but did not say so. Dos ten Han said the smaller ones could hardly go any distance in the dark. Bela ten Belen said nothing, but took out the long lace from one of his sandals and tied one end around the neck of the little girl he had taken and the other end around his own wrist; then he made the child lie down, and lay down to sleep next to her. Her sister, the one who had followed them, lay down by her on the other side. Bela said, "Dos, keep watch first, then wake me."

So the night passed. The children did not try to escape, and no one came on their trail. The next day they kept going south but mainly west, so that by midafternoon they reached the Dayward Hills. They children walked, even the five-year-old, and the men passed the two babies from one to another, so their pace was steady if not fast. Along in the morning, the marsh-fire girl pulled at Bela's tunic and kept pointing left, to a swampy place, making gestures of pulling up roots and eating. Since they had eaten nothing for two days, they followed her. The older children waded out into the water and pulled up certain wide-leaved plants by the roots. They began to cram what they pulled up into their mouths, but the soldiers waded after them and took the muddy roots and ate them till they had had enough. Dirt people do not eat before Crown people eat. The children did not seem surprised.

When she had finally got and eaten a root for herself, the marsh-fire girl pulled up another, chewed some and spat it out into her hand for the babies to eat. One of them ate eagerly from her hand, but the other would not;

she lay where she had been put down, and her eyes did not seem to see. Dos ten Han's girl and the marsh-fire girl tried to make her drink water. She would not drink.

Dos stood in front of them and said, pointing to the elder girl, "Vui Handa," naming her Vui and saying she belonged to his family. Bela named the marsh-fire girl Modh Belenda, and her little sister, the one he had carried off, he named Mal Belenda. The other men named their prizes, but when Ralo ten Bal pointed at the sick baby to name her, the marsh-fire girl, Modh, got between him and the baby, vigorously gesturing no, no, and putting her hand to her mouth for silence.

"What's she up to?" Ralo asked. He was the youngest of the men, sixteen.

Modh kept up her pantomime: she lay down, lolled her head, and half opened her eyes, like a dead person; she leapt up with her hands held like claws and her face distorted, and pretended to attack Vui; she pointed at the sick baby.

The young men stood staring. It seemed she meant the baby was dying. The rest of her actions they did not understand.

Ralo pointed at the baby and said, "Groda," which is a name given to Dirt people who have no owner and work in the field teams—Nobody's.

"Come on," Bela ordered, and they made ready to go on. Ralo walked off, leaving the sick child lying.

"Aren't you bringing your Dirt?" one of the others asked him.

"What for?" he said.

Modh picked up the sick baby, Vui picked up the other baby, and they went on. After that the soldiers let the older girls carry the sick baby, though they themselves passed the well one about so as to make better speed.

When they got up on higher ground away from the clouds of stinging insects and the wet and heavy heat of the marshlands, the young men were glad, feeling they were almost safe now; they wanted to move fast and get back to the City. But the children, worn out, struggled to climb the steep hills. Vui, who was carrying the sick baby, straggled along slower and slower. Dos, her owner, slapped her legs with the flat of his sword to make her go faster. "Ralo, take your Dirt, we have to keep going," he said.

Ralo turned back angrily. He took the sick baby from Vui. The baby's face had gone greyish and its eyes were half closed, like Modh's in her pantomime. Its breath whistled a little. Ralo shook the child. Its head flopped. Ralo threw it away into the high bushes. "Come on, then," he said, and set off walking fast uphill.

Vui tried to run to the baby, but Dos kept her away from it with his sword, stabbing at her legs, and drove her on up the hill in front of him.

Modh dodged back to the bushes where the baby was, but Bela got in front of her and herded her along with his sword. As she kept dodging and trying to go back, he seized her by the arm, slapped her hard, and dragged her after him by the wrist. Little Mal stumbled along behind them.

When the place of the high bushes was lost from sight behind a hillslope, Vui began to make a shrill long-drawn cry, a keening, and so did Modh and Mal. The keening grew louder. The soldiers shook and beat them till they stopped but soon they started again, all the children, even the baby. The soldiers did not know if they were far enough from the nomads and near enough the Fields of the City that they need not fear pursuers hearing the sound. They hurried on, carrying or dragging or driving the children, and the shrill keening cry went with them like the sound of the insects in the marshlands.

It was almost dark when they got to the crest of the Dayward Hills. Forgetting how far south they had gone, the men expected to look down on the Fields and the City. They saw only dusk falling lands, and the dark west, and the lights of the City of the Sky beginning to shine.

They settled down in a clearing, for all were very tired. The children huddled together and were asleep almost at once. Bela forbade the men to make fire. They were hungry, but there was a creek down the hill to drink from. Bela set Ralo ten Bal on first watch. Ralo was the one who had gone to sleep, their first night out, allowing Bidh to escape.

Bela woke in the night, cold, missing his cape, which he had torn up to make bonds. He saw that someone had made a small fire and was sitting cross-legged beside it. He sat up and said "Ralo!" furiously, and then saw that the man was not Ralo but the guide, Bidh.

Ralo lay motionless near the fire.

Bela drew his sword.

"He fell asleep again," the Dirt man said, grinning at Bela.

Bela kicked Ralo, who snorted and sighed and did not wake. Bela leapt up and went round to the others, fearing Bidh had killed them in their sleep, but they had their swords and were sleeping soundly. The children slept in a little heap. He returned to the fire and stamped it out.

"Those people are miles away," Bidh said. "They won't see the fire. They never found your track."

"Where did you go?" Bela asked him after a while, puzzled and suspicious. He did not understand why the Dirt man had come back.

"To see my people in the village."

"Which village?"

"The one nearest the hills. My people are the Allulu. I saw my grandfather's hut from up in the hills. I wanted to see the people I used to know. My mother's still alive, but my father and brother have gone to the Sky City. I talked with my people and told them a foray was coming. They waited for you in their huts. They would have killed you, but you would have killed some of them. I was glad you went on to the Tullu village."

It is fitting that a Crown ask a Dirt person questions, but not that he converse or argue with him. Bela, however, was so disturbed that he said sharply, "Dead Dirt does not go to the Sky City. Dirt goes to dirt."

"So it is," Bidh said politely, as a slave should, with his fist to his forehead. "My people foolishly believe that they go to the sky, but even if they did, no doubt they wouldn't go to the palaces there. No doubt they wander in the wild, dirty parts of the sky." He poked at the fire to see if he could start a flame, but it was dead. "But you see, they can only go up there if they have been buried. If they're not buried, their soul stays down here on earth. It's likely to turn into a very bad thing then. A bad spirit. A ghost."

"Why did you follow us?" Bela demanded.

Bidh looked puzzled, and put his fist to his forehead. "I belong to Lord ten Han," he said. "I eat well, and live in a fine house. I'm respected in the City because of my sister and being a guide. I don't want to stay with the Allulu. They're very poor."

"But you ran away!"

"I wanted to see my family," Bidh said. "And I didn't want them to be killed. I only would have shouted to them to warn them. But you tied my legs. That made me so sad. You failed to trust me. I could think only about my people, and so I ran away. I am sorry, my lord."

"You would have warned them. They would have killed us!"

"Yes," Bidh said, "if you'd gone there. But if you'd let me guide you, I would have taken you to the Bustu or the Tullu village and helped you catch children. Those are not my people. I was born an Allulu and am a man of the City. My sister's child is a god. I am to be trusted."

Bela ten Belen turned away and said nothing.

He saw the starlight in the eyes of a child, her head raised a little, watching and listening. It was the marsh-fire girl, Modh, who had followed them to be with her sister.

"That one," Bidh said. "That one, too, will mother gods."

II

CHERGO'S DAUGHTER AND DEAD AYU'S First Daughter, who were now named Vui and Modh, whispered in the grey of the morning before the men woke.

"Do you think she's dead?" Vui whispered.

"I heard her crying. All night."

They both lay listening.

"That one named her," Vui whispered very low. "So she can follow us."

"She will."

The little sister, Mal, was awake, listening. Modh put her arm around her and whispered, "Go back to sleep."

Near them, Bidh suddenly sat up, scratching his head. The girls stared wide-eyed at him.

"Well, Daughters of Tullu," he said in their language, spoken the way the Allulu spoke it, "you're Dirt people now."

They stared and said nothing.

"You're going to live in heaven on earth," he said. "A lot of food. Big, rich huts to live in. And you don't have to carry your house around on your back across the world! You'll see. Are you virgins?"

After a while they nodded.

"Stay that way if you can," he said. "Then you can marry gods. Big, rich husbands! These men are gods. But they can only marry Dirt women. So look after your little cherrystones, keep them from Dirt boys and men like me, and then you can be a god's wife and live in a golden hut."

He grinned at their staring faces and stood up to piss on the cold ashes of the fire.

While the Crown men were rousing, Bidh took the older girls into the forest to gather berries from a tangle of bushes nearby; he let them eat some, but made them put most of what they picked into his cap. He brought the cap full of berries back to the soldiers and offered them, his knuckles to his forehead. "See," he said to the girls, "this is how you must do. Crown people are like babies and you must be their mothers."

Modh's little sister Mal and the younger children were silently weeping with hunger. Modh and Vui took them to the stream to drink. "Drink all you can, Mal," Modh told her sister. "Fill up your belly. It helps." Then she said to Vui, "Man-babies!" and spat. "Men who take food from children!"

"Do as the Allulu says," said Vui.

Their captors now ignored them, leaving Bidh to look after them. It was some comfort to have a man who spoke their language with them. He was kind enough, carrying the little ones, sometimes two at a time, for he was strong. He told Vui and Modh stories about the place where they were going. Vui began to call him Uncle. Modh would not let him carry Mal, and did not call him anything.

Modh was eleven. When she was six, her mother had died in childbirth, and she had always looked after the little sister.

When she saw the golden man pick up her sister and run down the hill, she ran after them with nothing in her mind but that she must not lose the little one. The men went so fast at first that she could not keep up, but she did not lose their trace, and kept after them all that day. She had seen her grandmothers and grandfathers slaughtered like pigs. She thought everybody she knew in the world was dead. Her sister was alive and she was alive. That was enough. That filled her heart.

When she held her little sister in her arms again, that was more than enough.

But then, in the hills, the cruel man named Sio's Daughter and then threw her away, and the golden man kept her from going to pick her up. She tried to look back at the high bushes where the baby lay, she tried to see the place so she could remember it, but the golden man hit her so she was dizzy and drove and dragged her up the hill so fast her breath burned in her chest and her eyes clouded with pain. Sio's Daughter was lost. She would lie dead there in the bushes. Foxes and wild dogs would eat her flesh and break her bones. A terrible emptiness came into Modh, a hollow, a hole of fear and anger that everything else fell into. She would never be able to go back and find the baby and bury her. Children before they are named have no ghosts, even if they are unburied, but the cruel one had named Sio's Daughter. He had pointed and named her: Groda. Groda would follow them. Modh had heard the thin cry in the night. It came from the hollow place. What could fill that hollow? What could be enough?

III

BELA TEN BELEN AND HIS COMPANIONS did not return to the City in triumph, since they had not fought with other men; but neither did they have to creep in by back ways at night as an unsuccessful foray. They had not lost a man, and they brought back six slaves, all female. Only Ralo ten Bal brought nothing, and the others joked about him losing his catch and falling asleep on watch. And Bela ten Belen joked about his own luck in catching two fish on one hook, telling how the marsh-fire girl had followed them of her own will to be with her sister.

As he thought about his foray, he realized that they had been lucky indeed, and that their success was due not to him, but to Bidh. If Bidh had told them to do so, the Allulu would have ambushed and killed the soldiers before they ever reached the farther village. The slave had saved them. His loyalty seemed natural and expectable to Bela, but he honored it. He knew Bidh and his sister Nata were fond of each other, but could rarely see each other, since Bidh belonged to the Hans and Nata to the Belens. When the opportunity arose, he traded two of his own house-slaves for Bidh and made him overseer of the Belen House slave compound.

Bela had gone slave-catching because he wanted a girl to bring up in the house with his mother and sister and his brother's wife: a young girl, to be trained and formed to his desire until he married her.

Some Crown men were content to take their Dirt wife from the dirt, from the slave quarters of their own compound or the barracks of the city, to get children on her, keep her in the hanan, and have nothing else to do with her. Others were more fastidious. Bela's mother Hehum had been brought up from birth in a Crown hanan, trained to be a Crown's wife. Nata, four years old when she was caught, had lived at first in the slave barracks, but within a few years a Root merchant, speculating on the child's beauty, had traded five male slaves for her and kept her in his hanan so that she would not be raped or lie with a man till she could be sold as a wife. Nata's beauty became famous, and many Crown men sought to marry her. When she was fifteen, the Belens traded the produce of their best field and the use of a whole building in Copper Street for her. Like her mother-in-law, she was treated with honor in the Belen household.

Finding no girl in the barracks or hanans he was willing to look at as a wife, Bela had resolved to go catch a wild one. He had succeeded doubly.

At first he thought to keep Mal and send Modh to the barracks. But though Mal was charming, with a plump little body and big, long-lashed eyes, she was only five years old. He did not want sex with a baby, as some men did. Modh was eleven, still a child, but not for long. She was not always beautiful, but always vivid. Her courage in following her sister had impressed him. He brought both sisters to the hanan of the Belen house and asked his mother, his sister-in-law, and his sister to see that they were properly brought up.

It was strange to the wild girls to hear Nata Belenda speak words of their language, for to them she seemed a creature of another order, as did Hehum Belenda, the mother of Bela and Alo, and Tudju Belen, the sister. All three women were tall and clean and soft-skinned, with soft hands and long lustrous hair. They wore garments of cobweb colored like spring flowers, like sunset clouds. They were goddesses. But Nata Belenda smiled and was gentle and tried to talk to the children in their own tongue, though she remembered little of it. The grandmother Hehum Belenda was grave and stern-looking, but quite soon she took Mal onto her lap to play with Nata's baby boy. Tudju, the daughter of the house, was the one who most amazed them. She was not much older than Modh, but a head taller, and Modh thought she was wearing moonlight. Her robes were cloth of silver, which only Crown women could wear. A heavy silver belt slanted from her waist to her hip, with a marvelously worked silver sheath hanging from it. The sheath was empty, but she pretended to draw a sword from it, and flourished the sword of air, and lunged with it, and laughed to see little Mal still looking for the sword. But she showed the girls that they must not touch her; she was sacred, that day. They understood that.

Living with these women in the great house of the Belens, they began to understand many more things. One was the language of the City. It was not so different from theirs as it seemed at first, and within a few weeks they were babbling along in it.

After three months they attended their first ceremony at the Great Temple: Tudju's coming of age. They all went in procession to the Great Temple. To Modh it was wonderful to be out in the open air again, for she was weary of walls and ceilings. Being Dirt women, they sat behind the yellow curtain, but they could see Tudju chose her sword from the row of swords hanging behind the altar. She would wear it the rest of her life whenever she went out of the house. Only women born to the Crown wore swords. No one else in the City was allowed to carry any weapon, except Crown men when they served as soldiers. Modh and Mal knew that, now. They knew many things, and also knew there was much more to learn—everything one had to know to be a woman of the City.

It was easier for Mal. She was young enough that to her the City rules and ways soon became the way of the world. Modh had to unlearn the rules and ways of the Tullu people. But as with the language, some things were more familiar than they first seemed. Modh knew that when a Tullu man was elected chief of the village, even if he already had a wife he had to marry a slave woman. Here, the Crown men were all chiefs. And they all had to marry Dirt women—slaves. It was the same rule, only, like everything in the City, made greater and more complicated.

In the village, there had been two kinds of person, Tullu and slaves. Here there were three kinds; and you could not change your kind, and you could not marry your kind. There were the Crowns, who owned land and slaves, and were all chiefs, priests, gods on earth. And the Dirt people, who were slaves. Even though a Dirt woman who married a Crown might be treated almost like a Crown herself—like the Nata and Hehum—still, they were Dirt. And there were the other people, the Roots.

Modh knew little about the Roots. There was nobody like them in her village. She asked Nata about them and observed what she could from the seclusion of the hanan. Root people were rich. They oversaw planting and harvest, the storehouses and marketplaces. Root women were in charge of housebuilding, and all the marvelous clothes the Crowns wore were made by Root women.

Crown men had to marry Dirt women, but Crown women, if they married, had to marry Root men. When she got her sword, Tudju also acquired several suitors— Root men who came with packages of sweets and stood outside the hanan curtain and said polite things, and then went and talked to Alo and Bela, who were the lords of Belen since their father had died in a foray years ago.

Root women had to marry Dirt men. There was a Root woman who wanted to buy Bidh and marry him. Alo and Bela told him they would sell him or keep him, as he chose. He had not decided yet.

Root people owned slaves and crops, but they owned no land, no houses. All real property belonged to Crowns. "So," said Modh, "Crowns let the Root people live in the City, let them have this house or that, in exchange for the work they do and what their slaves grow in the fields—is that right?"

"As a reward for working," Nata corrected her, always gentle, never scolding. "The Sky Father made the City for his sons, the Crowns. And they reward good workers by letting them live in it. As our owners, Crowns and Roots, reward us for work and obedience by letting us live, and eat, and have shelter."

Modh did not say, "But—"

It was perfectly clear to her that it was a system of exchange, and that it was not fair exchange. She came from just far enough outside it to be able to look at it. And, being excluded from reciprocity, any slave can see the system with an undeluded eye. But Modh did not know of any other system, any possibility of another system, which would have allowed her to say "But." Neither did Nata know of that alternative, that possible even when unattainable space in which there is room for justice, in which the word "But" can be spoken and have meaning.

Nata had undertaken to teach the wild girls how to live in the City, and she did so with honest care. She taught them the rules. She taught them what was believed. The rules did not include justice, so she did not teach them justice. If she did not herself believe what was believed, yet she taught them how to live with those who did. Modh was self-willed and bold when she came, and Nata could easily have let her think she had rights, encouraged her to rebel, and then watched her be whipped or mutilated or sent to the fields to be worked to death. Some slave women would have done so. Nata, kindly treated most of her life, treated others kindly. Warm-hearted, she took the girls to her heart. Her own baby boy was a Crown, she was proud of her godling, but she loved the wild girls too. She liked to hear Bidh and Modh talk in the language of the nomads, as they did sometimes. Mal had forgotten it by then.

Mal soon grew out of her plumpness and became as thin as Modh. After a couple of years in the City both girls were very different from the tough little wildcats Bela ten Belen's foray had caught. They were slender, delicate-looking. They ate well and lived soft. These days, they might not have been able to keep up the cruel pace of their captors' flight to the City. They got little exercise but dancing, and had no work to do. Conservative Crown families like the Belens did not let their slave wives do work that was beneath them, and all work was beneath a Crown.

Modh would have gone mad with boredom if the grandmother had not let her run and play in the courtyard of the compound, and if Tudju had not taught her to sword-dance and to fence. Tudju loved her sword and the art of using it, which she studied daily with an older priestess. Equipping Modh with a blunted bronze practice sword, she passed along all she learned, so as to have a partner to practice with. Tudju's sword was extremely sharp, but she already used it skillfully and never once hurt Modh.

Tudju had not yet accepted any of the suitors who came and murmured at the yellow curtain of the hanan. She imitated the Root men mercilessly after they left, so that the hanan rocked with laughter. She claimed she could smell each one coming—the one that smelled like boiled chard, the one that smelled like cat-dung, the one that smelled like old men's feet. She told Modh, in secret, that she did not intend to marry, but to be a priestess and a judge-councillor. But she did not tell her brothers that. Bela and Alo were expecting to make a good profit in food-supply or clothing from Tudju's marriage; they lived expensively, as Crowns should. The Belen larders and clothes-chests had been supplied too long by bartering rentals for goods. Nata alone had cost twenty years' rent on their best property.

Modh made friends among the Belenda slaves and was very fond of Tudju, Nata, and old Hehum, but she loved no one as she loved Mal. Mal was all she had left of her old life, and she loved in her all that she had lost for her. Perhaps Mal had always been the only thing she had: her sister, her child, her charge, her soul.

She knew now that most of her people had not been killed, that her father and the rest of them were no doubt following their annual round across the plains and hills and waterlands; but she never seriously thought of trying to escape and find them. Mal had been taken, she had followed Mal. There was no going back. And as Bidh had said to them, it was a big, rich life here.

She did not think of the grandmothers and grandfathers lying slaughtered, or Dua's Daughter who had been beheaded. She had seen all that yet not seen it; it was her sister she had seen. Her father and the others would have buried all those people and sung the songs for them. They were here no longer. They were going on the bright roads and the dark roads of the sky, dancing in the bright hut-circles up there.

She did not hate Bela ten Belen for leading the raid, killing Dua's Daughter, stealing her and Mal and the others. Men did that, nomads as well as City men. They raided, killed people, took food, took slaves. That was the way men were. It would be as stupid to hate them for it as to love them for it.

But there was one thing that should not have been, that should not be and yet continued endlessly to be, the small thing, the nothing that when she remembered it made the rest, all the bigness and richness of life, shrink up into the shriveled meat of a bad walnut, the yellow smear of a crushed fly.

It was at night that she knew it, she and Mal, in their soft bed with cobweb sheets, in the safe darkness of the warm, high-walled house: Mal's indrawn breath, the cold chill down her own arms, do you hear it?

They clung together, listening, hearing.

Then in the morning Mal would be heavy-eyed and listless, and if Modh tried to make her talk or play she would begin to cry, and Modh would sit down at last and hold her and cry with her, endless, useless, dry, silent weeping. There was nothing they could do. The baby followed them because she did not know whom else to follow.

Neither of them spoke of this to anyone in the household. It had nothing to do with these women. It was theirs. Their ghost.

Sometimes Modh would sit up in the dark and whisper aloud, "Hush, Groda! Hush, be still!" And there might be silence for a while. But the thin wailing would begin again.

Modh had not seen Vui since they came to the City. Vui belonged to the Hans, but she had not been treated as Modh and Mal had. Dos ten Han bargained for a pretty girl from a Root wife-broker, and Vui was one of the slaves he bartered for that wife. If she was still alive, she did not live where Modh could reach her or hear of her. Seen from the hills, as she had seen it that one time, the City did not look very big in the great slant and distance of the fields and meadows and forests stretching on to the west; but if you lived in it, it was as endless as the plains. You could be lost in it. Vui was lost in it.

Modh was late coming to womanhood, by City standards: fourteen. Hehum and Tudju held the ceremony for her in the worship-room of the house, a full day of rituals and singing. She was given new clothes. When it was over Bidh came to the yellow curtain of the hanan, called to her, and put into her hands a little deerskin pouch, crudely stitched.

She looked at it puzzled. Bidh said, "You know, in the village, a girl's uncle gives her a delu," and turned away. She caught his hand and thanked him, touched, half-remembering the custom and fully knowing the risk he had run in making his gift. Dirt people were forbidden to do any sewing. Sewing was a Root prerogative. A slave found with a needle and thread could have a hand cut off. Like his sister Nata, Bidh was warm-hearted. Both Modh and Mal had called him Uncle for years now.

Alo ten Belen had three sons from Nata by now to be priests and soldiers of the House of Belen. Alo came most nights to play with the little boys and take Nata off to his rooms, but they saw little of Bela in the hanan. His friend Dos ten Han had given him a concubine, a pretty, teasing, experienced woman who kept him satisfied for a long time. He had forgotten about the nomad sisters, lost interest in his plans of educating them. Their days passed peacefully and cheerfully. As the years went by, their nights too grew more peaceful. The crying now came seldom to Modh, and only in a dream, from which she could waken.

But always, when she wakened so, she saw Mal's eyes wide open in the darkness. They said nothing, but held each other till they slept again.

In the morning, Mal would seem quite herself; and Modh would say nothing, fearing to upset her sister, or fearing to make the dream no dream.

Then things changed.

Tudju's brothers Bela and Alo called for her. She was gone all day, and came back to the hanan looking fierce and aloof, fingering the hilt of her silver sword. When her mother went to embrace her, Tudju made the gesture that put her aside. All these years with Tudju in the hanan, it had been easy to forget that she was a Crown woman, the only Crown among them; that the yellow curtain was to separate them, not her, from the sacred parts of the house;

that she was herself a sacred being. But now she had to take up her birthright.

"They want me to marry that fat Root man, so we can get his shop and looms in Silk Street," she said. "I will not. I am going to live at the Great Temple." She looked around at them all, her mother, her sister-in-law, Mal, Modh, the other slave women. "Everything I'm given there, I'll send here," she said. "But I told Bela that if he gives one finger's width of land for that woman he wants now, I'll send nothing home from the Temple. He can go slave-catching again to feed her. And you." She looked again at Mal and Modh. "Keep an eye on him," she said. "It is time he married."

Bela had recently traded his concubine and the Dirt son she had borne him, making a good bargain in cropland, and then promptly offered almost the whole amount for another woman he had taken a fancy to. It was not a question of marriage, for a Dirt woman, to marry, must be a virgin, and the woman he wanted had been owned by several men. Alo and Tudju had prevented the bargain, which he could not make without their consent. It was, as Tudju said, time for Bela to consider his sacred obligation to marry and beget children of the sky on a woman of the dirt.

So Tudju left the hanan and the house to serve in the Great Temple, only returning sometimes on formal visits. She was replaced, evenings, by her brother Bela. Dour and restless, like a dog on a chain, he would stalk in after Alo, and watch the little boys running about and the slaves' games and dances.

He was a tall man, handsome, lithe and well muscled. From the day she first saw him in the horror and carnage of the foray, to Modh he had been the golden man. She had seen many other golden men in the City since then, but he was the first, the model.

She had no fear of him, other than the guardedness a slave must feel towards the master; he was spoilt, of course, but not capricious or cruel; even when he was sulky he did not take out his temper on his slaves. Mal, however, shrank from him in uncontrollable dread. Modh told her she was foolish. Bela was nearly as good-natured as Alo, and Mal trusted Alo completely. Mal just shook her head. She never argued, and grieved bitterly when she disagreed with her sister on anything, but she could not even try not to fear Bela.

Mal was thirteen. She had her ceremony (and to her too Bidh secretly gave a crude little "soulbag"). In the evening of that day she wore her new clothing. Dirt people even when they lived with Crowns could not wear sewn garments, only lengths of cloth; but there are many graceful ways of draping and gathering unshaped material, and though the spidersilk could not be hemmed, it could be delicately fringed and tasseled. Mal's garments were undyed silk, with a blue-green overveil so fine it was transparent.

When she came in, Bela looked up, and looked at her, and went on looking.

Modh stood up suddenly without plan or forethought and said, "Lords, Masters! May I dance for my sister's festival?" She scarcely waited for their consent, but spoke to Lui, who played the tablet-drums for dancers, and ran to her room for the bronze sword Tudju had given her and the pale flame-colored veil that had been given her at her festival. She ran back with the veil flowing about her.

Lui drummed, and Modh danced. She had never danced so well. She had never danced the way she did now, with all the fierce formal precision of the sword-dance, but also with a wildness, a hint of threat in her handling of the blade, a sexual syncopation to the drumbeat that made Lui's drumming grow ever faster and fiercer in response, so that the dance gathered and gathered like a flame, hotter and brighter, the translucent veil flowing, whirling at the watchers' faces. Bela sat motionless, fixed, gazing, and did not flinch even when the veil struck its spiderweb blow across his eyes.

When she was done he said, "When did you learn to dance like that?"

"Under your eyes," she said.

He laughed, a little uneasy. "Let Mal dance now," he said, looking around for her.

"She's too tired to dance," Modh said. "The rites were long. She tires easily. But I will dance again."

He motioned her to go on dancing with a flick of his hand. She nodded to Lui, who grinned widely and began the hesitant, insinuating beat of the slow dance called mimei. Modh put on the ankle-bells Lui kept with her drums; she arranged her veil so that it covered her face and body and arms, baring only her ankles with the jingling anklets and her naked feet. The dance began, her feet moving slightly and constantly, her body swaying, the beat and the movements slowly becoming more intense.

She could see through the gauzy silk; she could see the stiff erection under Bela's silk tunic; she could see his heart beat in his chest.

After that night Bela hung around Modh so closely that her problem was not to draw his attention but to prevent his getting her alone and raping her. Hehum and the other women made sure she was never alone, for they were eager for Bela to marry her. They all liked her, and she would cost the House of Belen nothing. Within a few days Bela declared his intention to marry Modh. Alo gave his approval gladly, and Tudju came from the Temple to officiate at the marriage rites.

All Bela's friends came to the wedding. The yellow curtain was moved back from the dancing room, hiding only the sleeping rooms of the women.

For the first time in seven years Modh saw the men who had been on the foray. The man she remembered as the big one was Dos ten Han; Ralo ten Bal was the cruel one. She tried to keep away from Ralo, for the sight of him disturbed her. The youngest of the men, he had changed more than the others, yet he acted boyish and petulant. He drank a lot and danced with all the slave girls.

Mal hung back as always, and even more than usual; she was frightened without the yellow curtain to hide behind, and the sight of the men from the foray made her tremble. She tried to stay close to Hehum. But the old woman teased her gently and pushed her forward to let the Crown men see her, for this was a rare chance to show her off. She was marriageable now, and these Crown men might pay to marry her rather than merely use her. She was very pretty, and might bring back a little wealth to the Belens.

Modh pitied her misery, but did not worry about her safety even among drunken men. Hehum and Alo would not let anybody have her virginity, which was her value as a bride.

Bela stayed close beside Modh every moment except when she danced. She danced two of the sword dances and then the mimei. The men watched her breathlessly, while Bela watched her and them, tense and triumphant. "Enough!" he said aloud just before the end of the veiled dance, perhaps to prove he was master even of this flame of a woman, perhaps because he could not restrain himself. She stopped instantly and stood still, though the drum throbbed on for a few beats.

"Come," he said. She put out her hand from the veil, and he took it and led her out of the great hall, to his apartments. Behind them was laughter, and a new dance began.

It was a good marriage. They were well matched. She was wise enough to obey any order he gave immediately and without any resistance, but she never forestalled his orders by anticipating his wishes, babying him, coddling him, as most slave women he knew had done. He felt in her an unyieldingness that allowed her to be obedient yet never slavish. It was as if in her soul she were indifferent to him, no matter what their bodies did; he could bring her to sexual ecstasy or, if he liked, he could have had her tortured, but nothing he did would change her, would touch her; she was like a wildcat or a fox, not tameable.

This impassibility, this distance kept him drawn to her, trying to lessen it. He was fascinated by her, his little fox, his vixen. In time they became friends as well. Their lives were boring; they found each other good company.

In the daytime, he was off, of course, still sometimes playing in the ballcourts with his friends, performing his priestly duties at the temples, and increasingly often going to the Great Temple. Tudju wanted him to join the Council. She had a considerable influence over Bela, because she knew what she wanted and he did not. He never had known what he wanted. There was not much for a Crown man to want. He had imagined himself a soldier until he led the foray over the Dayward Hills. Successful as it had been, in that they had caught slaves and come home safe, he could not bear to recall the slaughter, the hiding, the proof of his own ineptitude, the days and nights of fear, confusion, disgust, exhaustion, and shame. So there was nothing to do but play in the ballcourts, officiate at rites, and drink, and dance. And now there was Modh. And sons of his own to come. And maybe, if Tudju kept at him, he would become a councillor. It was enough.

For Modh, it was hard to get used to sleeping beside the golden man and not beside her sister. She would wake in darkness, and the weight of the bed and the smell and everything was wrong. She would want Mal then, not him. But in the daytime she would go back to the hanan and be with Mal and the others just as before, and then he would be there in the evening, and it would have been all right, it would have been good, except for Ralo ten Bal.

Ralo had noticed Mal on the wedding night, cowering near Hehum, in her blue veil that was like a veil of rain. He had come up to her and tried to make her talk or dance; she had shrunk, quailed, shivered. She would not speak or look up. He put his thumb under her chin to make her raise her face, and at that Mal retched as if about to vomit and staggered where she stood. Hehum had interfered: "Lord Master ten Bal, she is untouched," she said, with the stern dignity of her position as Mother of Gods. Ralo laughed and withdrew his hand, saying foolishly, "Well, I've touched her now."

Within a few days an offer for her had come from

the Bals. It was not a good one. She was asked for as a slave girl, as if she were not marriageable, and the barter was to be merely the produce of one of the Bal grain-plots. Given the Bals' wealth and the relative poverty of the Belens, it was an insulting offer. Alo and Bela refused it without explanation or apology, haughtily. It was a great relief to Modh when Bela told her that. When the offer came, she had been stricken. Had she seduced Bela away from Mal only to leave her prey to a man Mal feared even more than Bela, and with better reason? Trying to protect her sister, had she exposed her to far greater harm? She rushed to Mal to tell her they had turned down the Bals' offer, and telling her burst into tears of guilt and relief. Mal did not weep; she took the good news quietly. She had been terribly quiet since the wedding.

She and Modh were together all day, as they had always been. But it was not the same; it could not be. The husband came between the sisters. They could not share their sleep.

Days and festivals passed. Modh had put Ralo ten Bal out of mind, when he came home with Bela after a game at the ballcourts. Bela did not seem comfortable about bringing him into the house, but had no reason to turn him away. Bela came into the hanan and said to Modh, "He hopes to see you dance again."

"You aren't bringing him behind the curtain?"

"Only into the dancing room."

He saw her frown, but was not accustomed to reading expressions. He waited for a reply.

"I will dance for him," Modh said.

She told Mal to stay back in the sleeping rooms in the hanan. Mal nodded. She looked small, slender, weary.

She put her arms around her sister. "Oh Modh," she said. "You're brave, you're kind."

Modh felt frightened and hateful, but she said nothing, only hugged Mal hard, smelling the sweet smell of her hair, and went back to the dancing room.

She danced, and Ralo praised her dancing. Then he said what she knew he had been waiting to say from the moment he came: "Where's your wife's sister, Bela?"

"Not well," Modh said, though it was not for a Dirt woman to answer a question one Crown asked another Crown.

"Not very well tonight," Bela said, and Modh could have kissed him from eyes to toes for hearing her, for saying it.

"Ill?"

"I don't know," Bela said, weakening, glancing at Modh.

"Yes," Modh said.

"But perhaps she could just come show me her pretty eyebrows."

Bela glanced at Modh again. She said nothing.

"I had nothing to do with that stupid message my father sent you about her," Ralo said. He looked from Bela to Modh and back at Bela, smirking, conscious of his power. "Father heard me talking about her. He just wanted to give me a treat. You must forgive him. He was thinking of her as an ordinary Dirt girl." He looked at Modh again. "Bring your little sister out just for a moment, Modh Belenda," he said, bland, vicious.

Bela nodded to her. She rose and went behind the yellow curtain.

She stood some minutes in the empty hall that led

to the sleeping rooms, then came back to the dancing room. "Forgive me, Lord Master Bal," she said in her softest voice, "the girl has a fever and cannot rise to obey your summons. She has been unwell a long time. I am so sorry. May I send one of the other girls?"

"No," Ralo said. "I want that one." He spoke to Bela, ignoring Modh. "You brought two home from that raid we went on. I didn't get one. I shared the danger, it's only fair you share the catch." He had evidently rehearsed this sentence.

"You got one," Bela said.

"What are you talking about?"

Bela looked uncomfortable. "You had one," he said, in a less decisive voice.

"I came home with nothing!" Ralo cried, his voice rising, accusing. "And you kept two! Listen, I know you've brought them up all these years, I know it's expensive rearing girls. I'm not asking for a gift."

"You very nearly did," Bela said, stiffly, in a low voice.

Ralo put this aside with a laugh. "Just keep in mind, Bela, we were soldiers together," he said, cajoling, boyish, putting his arm round Bela's shoulders. "You were my captain. I don't forget that! We were brothers in arms. Listen, I'm not talking about just buying the girl. You married one sister, I'll marry the other. Hear that? We'll be brothers in the dirt, how's that?" He laughed and slapped his hand on Bela's shoulder. "How's that?" he said. "You won't be the poorer for it, Captain!"

"This is not the time to talk about it," Bela said, awkward and dignified.

Ralo smiled and said, "But soon, I hope."

Bela stood, and Ralo had to take his leave. "Please send to tell me when Pretty Eyebrows is feeling better," he said to Modh, with his smirk and his piercing glance. "I'll come at once."

When he was gone Modh could not be silent. "Lord Husband, don't give Mal to him. Please don't give Mal to him."

"I don't want to," he said.

"Then don't! Please don't!"

"It's all his talk. He boasts."

"Maybe. But if he makes an offer?"

"Wait till he makes an offer," Bela said, a little heavily, but smiling. He drew her to him and stroked her hair. "How you fret over Mal. She's not really ill, is she?"

"I don't know. She isn't well."

"Girls," he said, shrugging. "You danced well tonight."

"I danced badly. I would not dance well for that scorpion."

That made him laugh. "You did leave out the best part of the amei."

"Of course I did. I want to dance that only for you."

"Lui has gone to bed, or I'd ask you to."

"Oh, I don't need a drummer. Here, here's my drum." She took his hands and put them on her full breasts. "Feel the beat?" she said. She stood, struck the pose, raised her arms, and began the dance, there right in front of him, till he seized her, burying his face between her thighs, and she sank down on him laughing.

Hehum came out into the dancing room; she drew back, seeing them, but Modh untangled herself from her husband and went to the old woman.

"Mal is ill," Hehum began, with a worried face.

"Oh I knew it, I knew it!" Modh cried, instantly certain that it was her fault, that her lie had made itself truth. She ran to Mal's room, which she shared with her so long.

Hehum followed her. "She hides her ears," she said, "I think she has the earache. She cries and hides her ears."

Mal sat up when Modh came into the room. She looked wild and haggard. "You hear it, you hear it, don't you?" she cried, taking Modh's hands.

"No," Modh murmured, "no, I don't hear it. I hear nothing. There is nothing, Mal."

Mal stared up at her. "When he comes," she whispered.

"No," Mal said.

"Groda comes with him."

"No. It was years ago, years ago. You have got to be strong, Mal, you have got to put all that away."

Mal let out a piteous, loud moan and put Modh's hands up over her own ears. "I don't want to hear it!" she cried, and began to sob violently.

"Tell my husband I will spend this night with Mal," Modh said to Hehum. She held her sister in her arms till she slept at last, and then she slept too, though not easily, waking often, listening always.

In the morning she went to Bidh and asked him if he knew what people—their people, the villagers—did about ghosts.

He thought about it. "I think if there was a ghost somewhere they didn't go there. Or they moved away. What kind of ghost?"

"An unburied person."

Bidh made a face. "They would move away," he said with certainty.

"What if it followed them?"

Bidh held out his hands. "I don't know! The priest, the yegug, would do something, I guess. Some spell. The yegug knew all about things like that. These priests here, these temple people, they don't know anything but their dances and singing and talk-talk-talk. So, what is this? Is it Mal?"

"Yes."

He made a face again. "Poor little one," he said. Then, brightening, "Maybe it would be good if she left this house."

Several days passed. Mal was feverish and sleepless, hearing the ghost cry or fearing to hear it every night. Modh spent the nights with her, and Bela made no objection. But one evening when he came home he talked some while with Alo, and then the brothers came to the hanan. Hehum and Nata were there with the children. The brothers sent the children away, and asked that Modh come. Mal stayed in her room.

"Ralo ten Bal wants Mal for his wife," Alo said. He looked at Modh, forestalling whatever she might say. "We said she is very young, and has not been well. He says he will not sleep with her until she is fifteen. He will have her looked after with every attention. He wants to marry her now so that no other man may compete with him for her."

"And so raise her price," Nata said, with unusual sharpness. She had been the object of such a bidding war, which was why the Belens had all but beggared themselves to buy her.

"The price the Bals offer now could not be matched by any house in the City," Alo said gravely. "Seeing we were unwilling, they at once increased what they offered, and increased it again. It is the largest bride-bargain I ever heard of. Larger than yours, Nata." He looked with a strange smile at his wife, half pride half shame, rueful, intimate. Then he looked at his mother and at Modh. "They offer all the fields of Nuila. Their western orchards. Five Root houses on Wall Street. The new silk factory. And gifts—jewelry, fine garments, gold." He looked down. "It is impossible for us to refuse," he said.

"We will be nearly as wealthy as we used to be," Bela said.

"Nearly as wealthy as the Bals," Alo said, with the same rueful twist to his mouth.

"They thought we were bargaining. It was ridiculous. Every time I began to speak, old Loho ten Bal would hold up his hand to stop me and add something to the offer!" He glanced at Bela, who nodded and laughed.

"Have you spoken to Tudju?" Modh said.

"Yes," Bela answered.

"She agrees?" The question was unnecessary. Bela nodded.

"Ralo will not mistreat your sister, Modh," Alo said seriously. "Not after paying such a price for her. He'll treat her like a golden statue. They all will. He is sick with desire for her. I never saw a man so infatuated. It's odd, he's barely seen her, only at your wedding. But he's enthralled."

"He wants to marry her right away?" Nata asked.

"Yes. But he won't touch her till she's fifteen. If we'd asked him he might have promised never to touch her at all!"

"Promises are easy," Nata said.

"If he does lie with her it won't kill her," Bela said. "It might do her good. She's been spoiled here. You spoil her, Modh. A man in her bed may be what she needs."

"But—*that man*—" Modh said, her mouth dry, her ears ringing.

"Ralo's a bit spoiled himself. There's nothing wrong with him."

"He—" She bit her lip. She could not say the words.

Bela was keeping her from turning back to pick up the baby, jabbing his sword at her, dragging her by the arm. Mal was crying and stumbling behind them in the dust, up the steep hill, among the trees.

They all sat in uncomfortable silence.

"So," Alo said, louder than necessary, "there will be another wedding."

"When?"

"Before the Sacrifice."

Another silence.

"We mean no harm to come to Mal," Alo said to Modh. "Be sure of that, Modh. Tell her that."

She sat unable to move or speak.

"Neither of you has ever been mistreated," Bela said, resentfully, as if answering an accusation. His mother frowned at him and clicked her tongue. He reddened and fidgeted.

"Go speak to your sister, Modh," Hehum said. Modh got up. As she stood she saw the walls and tapestries and faces grow small and bright, sparkling with little lights. She walked slowly and stopped in the doorway.

"I am not the one to tell her," she said, hearing her own voice far away.

"Bring her here then," Alo said.

She nodded; but when she nodded the walls kept turning around her, and reaching out for support, she fell in a half-faint.

Bela came to her and cradled her in his arms. "Little fox, little fox," he murmured. She heard him say angrily to Alo, "The sooner the better."

He carried Modh to their bedroom, sat with her till she pretended to sleep, then left her quietly.

She knew that by her concern, by the nights she had spent with Mal, she had let her husband become jealous of her sister.

It was for her sake I came to you! she cried to him in her heart.

But there was nothing she could say now that would not cause more harm.

When she got up she went to Mal's room. Mal ran to her weeping, but Modh only held her, not speaking, till the girl grew quieter. Then she said, "Mal, there is nothing I can do. You must endure this. So must I."

Mal drew back a little and said nothing for a while. "It cannot happen," she said then, with a kind of certainty. "It will not be allowed. The child will not allow it."

Modh was bewildered for a moment. She had for some days been fairly sure she was pregnant. Now she thought for a moment that Mal was pregnant. Then she understood.

"You must not think about that child," she said. "She was not yours or mine. She was not daughter or sister of ours. Her death was not our death."

"No. It is his," Mal said, and almost smiled. She stroked Modh's arms and turned away. "I will be good,

Modh," she said. "You must not let this trouble you— you and your husband. It's not your trouble. Don't worry. What must happen will happen."

Cowardly, Modh let herself accept Mal's reassurance. More cowardly still, she let herself be glad that it was only a few days until the wedding. Then what must happen would have happened. It would be done, it would be over.

She was pregnant; she told Hehum and Nata of the signs. They both smiled and said, "A boy."

There was a flurry of getting ready for the wedding. The ceremony was to be in Belen House, and the Belens refused to let the Bals provide food or dancers or musicians or any of the luxuries they offered. Tudju was to be the marriage priestess. She came a couple of days early to stay in her old home, and she and Modh played at sword-practice the way they had done as girls, while Mal looked on and applauded as she had used to do. Mal was thin and her eyes looked large, but she went through the days serenely. What her nights were, Modh did not know. Mal did not send for her. In the morning, she would smile at Modh's questions about the night and say, "It passed."

But the night before the wedding, Modh woke in the deep night, hearing a baby cry.

She felt Bela awake beside her.

"Where is that child?" he said, his voice rough and deep in the darkness.

She said nothing.

"Nata should quiet her brat," he said.

"It is not Nata's."

It was a thin, strange cry, not the bawling of Nata's healthy boys. They heard it first to the left, as if in the hanan. Then after a silence the thin wail came from their right, in the public rooms of the house.

"Maybe it's my child," Modh said.

"What child?"

"Yours."

"What do you mean?"

"I carry your child. Nata and Hehum say it's a boy. I think it's a girl, though."

"But why is it crying?" Bela whispered, holding her.

She shuddered and held him. "It's not our baby, it's not our baby," she cried.

All night the baby wailed. People rose up and lighted lanterns and walked the halls and corridors of Belen House. They saw nothing but each other's frightened faces. Sometimes the weak, sickly crying ceased for a long time, then it would begin again. Mostly it was faint, as if far away, even when it was heard in the next room. Nata's little boys heard it, and shouted, "Make it stop!" Tudju burned incense in the prayer room and chanted all night long. To her the faint wailing seemed to be under the floor, under her feet.

When the sun rose, the people of Belen House ceased to hear the ghost. They made ready for the wedding festival as best they could.

The people of Bal House came. Mal was brought out from behind the yellow curtain, wearing voluminous unsewn brocaded silks and golden jewelry, her transparent veil like rain about her head. She looked very small in the elaborate draperies, straight-backed, her gaze held down. Ralo ten Bal was resplendent in puffed and sequined velvet. Tudju lighted the wedding fire and began the rites.

Modh listened, listened, not to the words Tudju chanted. She heard nothing.

The wedding party was brief, strained, everything done with the utmost formality. The guests left soon after the ceremony, following the bride and groom to Bal House, where there was to be more dancing and music. Tudju and Hehum, Alo and Nata went with them for civility's sake. Bela stayed home. He and Modh said almost nothing to each other. They took off their finery and lay silent in their bed, taking comfort in each other's warmth, trying not to listen for the wail of the child. They heard nothing, only the others returning, and then silence.

Tudju was to return to the Temple the next day. Early in the morning she came to Bela and Modh's apartments. Modh had just risen.

"Where is my sword, Modh?"

"You put it in the box in the dancing room."

"Your bronze one is there, not mine."

Modh looked at her in silence. Her heart began to beat heavily.

There was a noise, shouting, beating at the doors of the house.

Modh ran to the hanan, to the room she and Mal had slept in, and hid in the corner, her hands over her ears.

Bela found her there later. He raised her up, holding her wrists gently. She remembered how he had dragged her by the wrists up the hill through the trees. "Mal killed Ralo," he said. "She had Tudju's sword hidden under her dress. They strangled her."

"Where did she kill him?"

"On her bed," Bela said bleakly. "He never did keep his promises."

"Who will bury her?"

"No one," Bela said, after a long pause. "She was a Dirt woman. She murdered a Crown. They'll throw her body in the butchers' pit for the wild dogs."

"Oh, no," Modh said. She slipped her wrists from his grip. "No," she said. "She will be buried."

Bela shook his head.

"Will you throw everything away, Bela?"

"There is nothing I can do," he said.

She leaped up, but he caught and held her.

He told the others that Modh was mad with grief. They kept her locked in the house, and kept watch over her.

Bidh knew what troubled her. He lied to her, trying to give her comfort; he said he had gone to the butcher's pit at night, found Mal's body, and buried it out past the Fields of the City. He said he had spoken what words he could remember that might be spoken to a spirit. He described Mal's grave vividly, the oak trees, the flowering bushes. He promised to take Modh there when she was well. She listened and smiled and thanked him. She knew he lied. Mal came to her every night and lay in the silence beside her.

Bela knew she came. He did not try to come to that bed again.

All through her pregnancy Modh was locked in Belen House. She did not go into labor until almost ten months had passed. The baby was too large; it would not be born, and with its death killed her.

Bela ten Belen buried his wife and unborn son with the Belen dead in the holy grounds of the Temple, for though she was only a Dirt woman, she had a dead god in her womb.

"STAYING AWAKE
WHILE WE READ"

LOOK OUT, BOOKS. You're dodos, again. Or anyhow turkeys. The Associated Press, using an AP-Ipsos poll of 1,003 adults and claiming an error margin of plus or minus 3% points (the kind of solemn statistic meant to silence such questions as which 1,003 adults? and what's the error margin of your error margin?) has announced that 27% of Americans haven't read a book all year.* Of those who did read, two-thirds cited the Bible and other religious works and barely half said they'd read anything describable as literature.

To reinforce the dire news the article refers to a 2004 NEA report that 43% of their respondents had spent a year entirely book-free. The NEA blamed the decline of reading on TV, movies, and the Internet. Understandably. We all know that the Average Adult American spends from sixteen to twenty-eight hours a day watching TV (my margin of error there may be a little broad) and the rest of the time ordering stuff from eBay and blogging.

---

*Alan Fram, "Books Get Low Rank on To-Do Lists," *The Oregonian*, August 22, 2007.

That we read so little appears to be newsworthy, even shocking, yet the tone of the article is almost congratulatory. The AP story quotes a project manager for a telecommunications company in Dallas: "I just get sleepy when I read," adding, "a habit with which millions of Americans doubtless can identify." Self-satisfaction with the inability to remain conscious when faced with printed matter seems misplaced. But I think the assumption—whether gloomy or faintly jubilant—of the imminent disappearance of reading is misplaced too.

The thing is, not very many people ever did read much. Why should we think they do, or ought to, now?

For a long, long time most people couldn't read at all. Literacy was not encouraged among the lower classes, laymen, or women. It was not only a demarcator between the powerful and the powerless, it was power itself. Pleasure was not an issue. The ability to maintain and understand commercial records, the ability to communicate across distance and in code, the ability to keep the word of God to yourself and transmit it only at your own will and in your own time—these are formidable means of control over others and aggrandizement of self. Every literate society began with literacy as a constitutive prerogative of the ruling class.

Only gradually, if at all, did writing-and-reading filter downward, becoming less sacred as it became less secret, and less directly potent as it became more popular. The Chinese Empire kept it as an effective tool of governmental control, basing advancement in the bureaucratic hierarchy strictly on a series of literary tests. The Romans, far less systematic, ended up letting slaves, women, and such rabble read and write; but they got their comeuppance from the religion-based society that succeeded them.

In the Dark Ages, to be a Christian priest usually meant you could read at least a little, but to be a layman meant you probably didn't, and to be almost any kind of woman meant you couldn't. Not only didn't, but couldn't—weren't allowed to. As in some Muslim societies today.

In the West, one can see the Middle Ages as a kind of slow broadening of the light of the written word, which brightens into the Renaissance, and shines out with Gutenberg. Then, before you know it, women slaves are reading and writing, and revolutions are made with pieces of paper called Declarations of this and that, and school-marms replace gunslingers all across the Wild West, and people are mobbing the steamer bringing the latest install-ment of a new novel to New York, crying, "Is Little Nell dead? Is she dead?"

I have no statistics to support what I am about to say (and if I did I wouldn't trust their margin of error) but it appears to me that the high point of reading in the United States was from the mid-nineteenth century to the mid-twentieth, with a kind of peak in the early twentieth. I think of the period as the century of the book. From around the 1850's on, as the public school came to be con-sidered fundamental to democracy, and as libraries went public and flourished, financed by local businessmen and multimillionaires, reading was assumed to be something we shared in common. And the central part of the curricu-lum from first grade on was "English," not only because immigrants wanted their children fluent in it, but because literature—fiction, scientific works, history, poetry—was a major form of social currency.

It's interesting, even a little scary, to look at old text-books, schoolbooks from the 1890's, 1900, 1910, like the

McGuffey's Readers of which a couple of battered copies still lay around the house when I was a child, or the *Fifty Famous Stories* (and *Fifty More Famous Stories*) from which my brothers and I, in the 1930's, learned much of what we still know about Western Civilization. The level both of literacy and of general cultural knowledge expected of a ten-year-old will almost certainly surprise you if you look at these books; it awed me a little even then.

On the evidence of such texts and of school curricula—for instance, the novels kids were expected to read in high school up through the 1960's—it appears that people really wanted and expected their children not only to be able to read, but to do it, and not to fall asleep doing it. Why?

Well, obviously, because literacy was pretty much the front door to any kind of individual economic advancement and class status; but also, I think, because reading was an important social activity. The shared experience of books was a genuine bond. To be sure, a person reading seems to be cut off from everything around them, almost as much as the person shouting banalities into a cell phone as they ram their car into your car. That's the private element in reading. But there is a large public one too, which consists in what you and others have read.

As people these days can maintain nonthreatening, unloaded, sociable conversation by talking about who's murdered whom on the latest big TV cop or mafia show, so strangers on the train or co-workers on the job in 1840 could talk perfectly unaffectedly together about *The Old Curiosity Shop* and whether poor Little Nell was going to cop it. Books provided a shared field of entertainment and enjoyment facilitating conversation. Since public school education, fairly standardized and also widely shared, was pretty heavy on poetry and various literary classics all through that period, a lot of people would recognize and enjoy a reference to or a quote from Tennyson, or Scott, or Shakespeare, those works being properties in common, a social meeting ground. A man might be less likely to boast about falling asleep at the sight of a Dickens novel than to feel left out of things by not having read it.

Even now literature keeps that social quality, for some; people do ask, "Read a good book lately?" And it is institutionalized, mildly, in book groups and in the popularity of bestsellers. Publishers get away with making dull, stupid, baloney-mill novels into bestsellers via mere PR, because people need bestsellers. It is not a literary need. It is a social need. We want books everybody is reading (and nobody finishes) so we can talk about them. Movies and TV don't fill quite the same slot, especially for women.

The occasional exception proves my rule: the genuine grassroots bestseller, like the first Harry Potter book. It hit a slot the PR people didn't even know existed: adults hungry for the kind of fantasy they'd stopped reading at ten. This was a readership Tolkien, despite his permanent bestsellerdom (an entirely different matter, unrecognized by the PR crowd), couldn't satisfy, because Tolkien's trilogy is for grownups, and these grownups didn't want grownup fantasy. They wanted a school story, where you can look down on outsiders because they're all despicable Muggles. And they wanted to talk to each other about it. When the kids really got in on it, this became the extraordinary phenomenon, fully exploited by the book's publishers of course but neither predictable nor truly manageable by them, exhibited in the excitement at the publication of each new book of the series. If we brought books over from England by ship these days, crowds would have swarmed on the docks of New York to greet the final volume, crying, "Did she kill him? Is he dead?" It was a genuine social phenomenon, as is the worship of rock stars and the whole subculture of popular music, which offers the adolescent/young adult both an exclusive in-group and a shared social experience. And it was about books.

I think that people have not talked enough about books as social vectors, and that publishers have been stupid in not at least trying to understand how they work. They never even noticed book clubs until Oprah goosed them.

But the stupidity of the contemporary, corporation-owned publishing company is fathomless. They think they can sell books as commodities.

Corporations are moneymaking entities controlled by obscenely rich executives and their anonymous accountants, which have acquired most previously independent publishing houses with the notion of making quick money by selling works of art and information.

I wouldn't be surprised to learn that such people "get sleepy when they read." But within the corporate whale are many luckless Jonahs who were swallowed alive with their old publishing house—editors and such anachronisms—people who read wide awake. Some of them are so alert they can scent out promising new writers. Some of them have their eyes so wide open they can even proofread. But it doesn't do them much good. For years now, most editors have had to waste most of their time on a very unlevel playing field, fighting Sales and Accounting. In those departments, beloved by the CEOs, a "good book" means a high gross and a "good writer" is one whose next book can be guaranteed to sell better than the last one. That there are no such writers is of no matter to the corporationeers, who don't comprehend fiction even if they run their lives by it. Their interest in books is self-interest, the profit that can be made out of them. Or occasionally, for the top execs, the Murdochs and other Merdles, the political power they can wield through them; but that is merely self-interest again, personal profit.

And not only profit. Growth. Capitalism As We Know It depends (as we know) on growth. The stockholder's holdings must increase yearly, monthly, daily, hourly. Capitalism is a body that judges its well-being by the size of its growth.

Endless growth, limitless growth, as in obesity? Or growth as in a lump on the skin or in the breast, cancer? The size of our growth is a strange way to judge our wellbeing.

The AP article used the word "flat"—book sales have been "flat" in recent years, it said. Smooth, in other words, like a healthy skin, or flat like a non-bulging belly? But no; fat's good, flat's bad. Just ask McDonald's.

Analysts attribute the listlessness to competition from the Internet and other media, the unsteady economy and a well-established industry with limited opportunity for expansion.

There's the trick: Expansion. The old publisher was quite happy if his supply and demand ran parallel, if he sold books steadily, "flatly." But how is a publisher to keep up the 10–20% annual growth in profits expected by the holy stockholder? How do you get book sales to expand endlessly, like the American waistline?

Michael Pollan's fascinating study in *The Omnivore's Dilemma* explains how you do it with corn. When you've grown enough corn to fill every reasonable demand, you create unreasonable demands—artificial needs. So, having induced the government to declare corn-fed beef to be the standard, you feed corn to cattle, who cannot digest corn, tormenting and poisoning them in the process. And you use the fats and sweets of corn byproducts to make an ever more bewildering array of soft drinks and fast foods, addicting people to a fattening yet inadequate, even damaging, diet in the process. And you can't stop the processes, because if you did profits might get "listless," or even "flat."

This system has worked only too well for corn, and indeed throughout American agriculture and manufacturing, which is why we increasingly eat junk and make junk while wondering why tomatoes in Europe taste like tomatoes and foreign cars are well engineered.

Hollywood bought into the system enthusiastically. The emphasis on "the Gross"—often the only thing you hear about a movie is how much money it grossed the first day, week, etc.—has enfeebled film-making to the point where there seem to be more remakes than anything else. A remake is supposed to be safe: it grossed before, so it will gross again. This is a predictably stupid way to do business involving an art form. Hollywood's growth-directed sellout is exceeded only by the modern fine-art market, where the price of a painting constitutes its entire value, and the most valued artist is one willing to make endless replications of safely trendy work.

You can cover Iowa border to border with Corn #2 and New York wall to wall with Warhols, but with books, you run into problems. Standardization of the product and its production can take you only so far. Maybe it's because there is some intellectual content to even the most brainless book. In reading, the mind is involved. People will buy interchangeable bestsellers, formula thrillers, romances, mysteries, pop biographies, hot-topic books—up to a point. But the product loyalty of readers is defective. Readers get bored. People who buy a canvas painted one solid color and entitled Blue #72 don't get bored with it because when they look at it they principally see the thousands of dollars it cost, and the canvas certainly makes no demand on the aesthetic sense or even on consciousness. But a book has to be read. It takes time. It takes effort. You have to be awake. And so you want some reward. The loyal fans bought *Death at One O'Clock* and *Death at Two O'Clock* . . . but all of a sudden they won't buy *Death at Eleven O'Clock* even though it's got exactly the same formula as all the others. Why? They got bored.

What is a good growth-capitalist publisher to do? Where can he be safe?

He can find some safety in exploiting the social function of literature. That includes the educational, of course—schoolbooks and college texts, a favorite prey of corporations—and also the bestsellers and popular books of fiction and nonfiction that provide a common current topic and a bond among people at work and in book clubs. Beyond that, I think the corporations are very foolish to look for either safety or continual growth in publishing books.

Even in my "century of the book," when it was taken for granted that many people read and enjoyed it, how many of them had or could make much time for reading once they were out of school? During those years most Americans worked hard and worked long hours. Weren't there always many who never read a book at all, and never very many who read a lot of books? If there never have been all that many people who read much, why do we think there should be now, or ever will be? Certainly the odds are that there won't be a 10–20% annual increase in their numbers.

If people made or make time to read, it's because it's part of their job, or because they have no access to other media—or because they enjoy reading. In all this lamenting and percentage-counting it's too easy to forget the people who simply love to read.

It moves me to know that a hardbitten Wyoming cowboy carried a copy of *Ivanhoe* in his saddlebag for thirty years, or that the mill girls of New England had Browning Societies.

Certainly, reading for pure pleasure became rarer as leisure time got filled up with movies and radio, then TV, then the Web; books are now only one of the entertainment media. When it comes to delivering actual entertainment, actual pleasure, though, they're not a minor one. The competition is dismal. Governmental hostility was emasculating public radio while Congress allowed a few corporations to buy out and debase private radio stations. TV has steadily lowered its standards of entertainment and art until most programs are either brain-numbing or actively nasty. Hollywood remakes remakes and tries to gross out, with an occasional breakthrough that reminds us what a movie can be when undertaken as art. And the Web offers everything to everybody, but perhaps because of that all-inclusion there is curiously little aesthetic satisfaction to be got from roaming on it. If you want the pleasure art gives, sure, you can look at pictures or listen to music or read a poem or a book on your computer: but those artifacts are made accessible by the Web, not created by it and not intrinsic to it. Perhaps blogging is an effort to bring creativity to networking, but most blogs are merely self-indulgent, and the best I've seen function only as good journalism. Maybe they'll develop aesthetic form, but they haven't yet. Nothing in the media provides pleasure as reliably as books do—if you like reading.

And a good many people do. Not a majority, but a steady minority.

And readers recognize their pleasure as different from that of simply being entertained. Viewing is often totally passive, reading is always an act. Once you've pressed the On button, TV goes on and on and on . . . you don't have to do anything but sit and stare. But you have to give a book your attention. You bring it alive. Unlike the other media, a book is silent. It won't lull you with surging music or deafen you with screeching laughtracks or fire gunshots in your livingroom. You can hear it only in your head. A book won't move your eyes for you like TV or a movie does. It won't move your mind unless you give it your mind, or your heart unless you put your heart in it. It won't do the work for you. To read a good novel well is to follow it, to act it, to feel it, to be-come it—everything short of writing it, in fact. Reading is a collaboration, an act of participation. No wonder not everybody is up to it.

Because they've put something of themselves into books, many people who read for pleasure have a particu-lar, often passionate sense of connection to them. A book is a thing, an artifact, not showy in its technology but complex and extremely efficient: a really neat little device, compact, pleasant to look at and handle, which can last decades, even centuries. Unlike a video or CD it does not have to be activated or performed by a machine; all it needs to activate it is light, a human eye, and a human mind. It is not one of a kind, and it is not ephemeral. It lasts. It is there. It is reliable. If a book told you something when you were fifteen, it will tell it to you again when you're fifty, though of course you may understand it so differently that it seems you're reading a whole new book.

This is important, the fact that a book is a thing, physically there, durable, indefinitely re-usable, an article of value.

In the durability of the book lies a great deal of what we call civilization. History begins with literacy: before the written word there is only archeology. The great part of what we know about ourselves, our past, and our world has long been contained in books. Judaism, Christianity, and Islam all center their faith in a book. The durability of books is a very great part of our continuity as an intelligent species. And so their willed destruction is seen as an ultimate barbarism. The burning of the Library of Alexandria has been remembered for two thousand years, as people may well remember the desecration and destruction of the great Library in Baghdad.

So to me one of the most despicable things about corporate publishing is their attitude that books are inherently worthless. If a title that was supposed to sell a lot doesn't "perform" within a few weeks, it gets the covers torn off or is pulped—trashed. The corporate mentality recognizes no success that is not immediate. It wants a blockbuster a week, and this week's blockbuster must eclipse last week's, as if there wasn't room for more than one book at a time. Hence the crass stupidity of corporate publishers in handling backlists.

Over the years, books kept in print may earn hundreds of thousands of dollars for their publisher and author. A few steady earners, even though the annual earnings are in what is now called "the midlist," can keep publishers in business for years, and even allow them to take a risk or two on new authors. If I were a publisher, I'd far rather own Tolkien than Rowling.

But "over the years" doesn't pay the holy stockholder's quarterly share and doesn't involve Growth. To get big quick money, the publisher must risk a multimillion-dollar advance to some author who's supposed to provide this week's bestseller. These multi-millions—often a dead loss—come out of funds that used to go to pay a normal advance to reliable midlist authors and pay the royalties on older books that kept selling. But the midlist authors have been dropped and the reliably selling older books remaindered, in order to feed Moloch.

Is that any way to run a business?

I keep hoping the corporations will realize that publishing is not, in fact, a sane or normal business with a nice healthy relationship to capitalism. The practices of literary publishing houses are, in almost every way, by normal business standards, impractical, exotic, abnormal, insane.

Parts of publishing are, or can be forced to be, successfully capitalistic: the textbook industry is all too clear a proof of that. And how-to books and that kind of thing have good market predictability. But inevitably some of what publishers publish is, or is partly, literature: art. And the relationship of art to capitalism is, to put it mildly, vexed. It is seldom a happy marriage. Amused contempt is about the pleasantest emotion either partner feels for the other. Their definitions of what profiteth a man are too different.

So why don't the corporations drop the literary publishing houses, or at least the literary departments of publishers they have bought, with amused contempt, as unprofitable? Why don't they let them go back to muddling along making just enough, in a good year, to pay the printers, the editors, modest advances and crummy royalties, and plowing most profits back into taking chances on new writers? There's no hope of creating new readers other than the kids coming up through the schools, who are no longer taught to read for pleasure and anyhow are distracted by electrons; not only is the relative number of readers unlikely to see any kind of useful increase, it may well keep shrinking. What's in this dismal scene for you, Mr. Corporate Executive? Why don't you just get out of it? Why don't you dump the ungrateful little pikers and get on with the real business of business, ruling the world?

Is it because you think if you own publishing you can control what's printed, what's written, what's read? Well, lotsa luck, sir. It's a common delusion of tyrants. Writers and readers, even as they suffer from it, regard it with amused contempt.

POEMS

The Next War

It will take place,
it will take time,
it will take life,
and waste them.

Peace Vigils

My friend, self, fool,
have you been standing
with a lighted candle
for five years
in the rain?
What for?

I guess to show
a candle can keep burning
in the rain.

Variations on an Old Theme

Boys and girls, come out to play,
The moon doth shine as bright as day.

Leave your supper and leave your sleep
And leave your playfellows in the street,
follow the roads that part and meet
over the hills to daybreak.

The moon goes down and the stars go in,
it's hard to see where your steps begin,
and dark behind lies the way you've been
over the hills to daybreak.

Long is the night and the journey far
down the roads where the lost towns are,
and there isn't a horse or a bus or a car
over the hills to daybreak.

You have to walk on your own foot-soles
with never a coat against the cold
and hardly a penny to pay the tolls
on the way to the hills at daybreak.

Barefoot, bare back, and empty hand
is how you come to the farther land
and see that country, when you stand
on the hills of home at daybreak.

The City of the Plain

What can I make it a metaphor for? This is transgression
made concrete and asphalt and 30-foot palms of
     aluminum.
This is the Gonetoofar. The Great Slot. A 3-D spectacular,
Moses meets Bambi in the technicolooliah desert yes Lord!
where pyramids tangle with hiltons, 4/5-size towers of eiffel
or possibly lego crouch under condos and blu-blu skies scraped
clean of all cloud, except for the yellowish forestfire
smoke from the mountains up yonder, actual mountains,
     5/5-size,
burning (but nobody's worried). Arable plains, or the lowlands,
my Spanish dictionary says it means, but not to the lady
     who crouches
hour after hour after hour in front of the videopokergame
inhaling the yellowish smoke of her camels, burning (but
nobody's worried), not to the lady who poledances,
not to the lady who lugs in the bucket and mops.
No: maybe to her, once. Not any more though. Lasvegas
are not any more in a language, is not what it says it is, has
nothing to mean. After lasvegas you have to go into the desert
for a long, for a long, for a long time. Years. Generations.

Envoi: to Lot's Wife

Salty lady dry your tears
nothing worth your sorrow
Salty lady don't look back
don't look back tomorrow

"THE CONVERSATION
OF THE MODEST"

OUR WORD *MODESTY* COMES FROM Latin *modestia,*
which is the opposite of *superbia*, pride: the moderate
as opposed to the overreaching, the overweening. To the
Romans modesty wasn't a negative, passive avoidance of
pride, but an active virtue requiring self-control and an
intelligent realism.

But it had a secondary, narrower, gendered sense.
For a woman, modesty meant quiet deference to one's male
superior/father/husband, plus a retiring manner designed
specifically not to attract the attention of other men.

This gendered connotation continued to encroach
on and weaken the larger meaning of the word. Most men,
and many women, don't consider a virtue supposed to be
proper to women to be praiseworthy in men. And when
Christianity came along, though Christian moralists called
pride a cardinal sin, its opposite wasn't modesty, but humility. Humbling oneself is quite a different matter from
avoiding arrogance. Humility is drastic, and often highly
visible. Modesty is nothing like so sexy as humility; inherently non-extreme, it consists largely in realistic assessment

of one's gifts and prospects, respect for probability, and distaste for swagger and boasting. You can show off your humility in quite dramatic ways, but modesty, by definition, doesn't and can't show off.

In the last century, the word went right out of fashion. It's seldom used now in a positive sense except as an adjective meaning unpretentious, mostly turning up as a euphemism for small or poor—a modest house, modest means.

Its direct opposite, immodesty, came to be applied mostly to female behavior and dress. I've never heard the word "immodest" applied to male costume, not even to something as preposterously boastful as a codpiece or as uncomfortably bulgeful as a ballet dancer's tights.

When women began to rebel against the gender hierarchy, the womanly virtues assigned by the hierarchs—silence, deference, obedience, passivity, timidity, modesty—of course came into question, and women began to disown them all with scorn. This process was well under way in the late nineteenth century, went on all through the twentieth, and continues now. Again a gendered interpretation overwhelmed the idea of modesty as a general attribute. As an admirable quality, as a human virtue, modesty is, at this point, pretty well dead.

This seems a pity.

So long as modesty was an unreasonable or humiliating demand for female self-suppression and asexual behavior, women might well scoff at and refuse it. But where is it now so enforced? In Islam, and in some conservative Christian sects and other religions, I suppose. Certainly not in Western society at large.

In the area of women's clothing, the notion of

modesty as a kind of limit to sexual flaunting and deliberate provocation exists mostly as an imaginary barrier which clothing designers keep lowering to titillate and raising a little again to tease. The appearance of physical modesty in fact has little to do with clothing, everything to do with convention. A naked woman can be completely modest in her demeanor, if nakedness is a norm in her society, while a fully dressed woman can appear as a flaunting, taunting sexual self-advertisement, if she wants to, or is expected to, or if the fashion in clothing forces it on her.

In the political arena, modesty has usually been rather a pose than a position. For most politicians, exhibitionism is the norm, sometimes with an effort to ground self-praise on an ethical basis, often showing only a shameless disregard for realistic self-judgment.

Advertising—boastfulness in the service of greed— is the great enemy of realistic assessment and respect for probability. Where profit is supposed to be unlimited, realistic assessment is unwanted. Advertising now sets the tone and style not only of politics but a great deal of what we say and do, read and hear. Thus strength of character is judged not by reliably competent behavior, but as a show of assertiveness, a display of aggressiveness. In order to prove that he's strong and confident, the president of the United States is required to talk about "kicking ass." The self-consciously vulgar, preening hostility of the term is the essence of its significance.

(I find the bumper-sticker slogan "Girls kick ass" particularly sad. What the slogan protests is the old notion of modest man-serving maidenhood, or the vicious demand that young Black women be humble and subservient. But such a vapid threat of indiscriminate violence fails as a protest: it doesn't evoke pride, it isn't a call to action, it's nothing but an advertising slogan.)

For an artist, insofar as modesty implies diffidence, an unwillingness to exhibit oneself or one's work, it's a virtue so dubious as to be a handicap. Art is a show, an exhibition. Self-doubt can smother a true gift, just as a canny self-confidence can parlay a minor talent into artistic fame. But if modesty is interpreted not as diffidence or self-effacingness, but as non-overweening, a realistic assessment of the job to be done and one's ability to do it, then you might say a chief virtue of excellent artists is their modesty. We may mistake it for arrogance because the ability they knew they had was so immense that they were unafraid to do what nobody else dared. But knowing your limits and going to them isn't arrogance. It's greatness of spirit. It leads to the immense, unboastful sureness of a Shakespeare or Rembrandt or Beethoven. Next to them the swagger artists, the great egos, the Wagners and Picassos, look a little smaller than life.

Self-advertisement by announcing the subversiveness of one's work, making a show of boldly overthrowing conventions long since overthrown, adopting a style for mere novelty, or in cynical mockery of an older style, or to shock—these are ploys artists first began using in the nineteenth century. They're common now, and particularly successful in architecture, painting, and sculpture. Writers and composers who attempt similar immodesties don't always meet with the complacent acceptance offered the visual artists.

Their prices are lower and their critics less collusive. The greatest work of art concerning modesty as a major character trait is the Jane Austen novel that people who adore *Emma* usually don't adore at all. The morality of the tale of an uppity girl getting brought down to size is simple, familiar, and welcome to everybody. The morality of *Mansfield Park* is not simple, is not familiar, and is unwelcome to those who consider extraversion a desirable norm and self-confidence an illimitable virtue. That a girl could really, truly, actually be modest—that is, assess her situation realistically, choose the behavior appropriate to it, and stick to it through immensely powerful opposition—to many readers seems so strange, even unnatural, that they can only dismiss her as a hypocrite. Fanny's fault is not falsity, but an undue lack of self-confidence, hardly surprising given her upbringing. Her realism fails; she misjudges herself. All the same, she sticks to reality as best she can, with a stubborn transparency of purpose that is the exact opposite of hypocrisy. I find her a fascinating, endearing, and true heroine.

It's my impression that people respond positively to modesty, and resent arrogance and overweening, though they'll endure a good deal of it without complaint, and are even impressed by it—probably because a great many people are, in fact, modest. They accept themselves as ordinary. They estimate their own worth without inflating it (or underestimating it, which leads to weakness and servility). They don't assume they have nothing to learn, so they're willing to listen. They lack the fatal conviction of innate superiority.

Therefore all too often they're willing to listen to people who pretend to superiority—the news commentators, the talk show shouters, the popes and priests and ayatollahs, the advertisers, the know-it-alls. Modesty's weak point is that it may permit arrogance in others. Its strong point is that in the long run arrogance doesn't fool it.

I think a great many people still hold modesty to be a virtue and practice it, even if they don't use the word. I'm thinking of everyday conversations—carpenters working together on a job, secretaries chatting during a break, people having a beer or dinner together and talking about whatever they're interested in and know about. It appears to me that in these situations, modesty of demeanor is the norm. Overbearing garrulity about my sweet deal on the Honda, my trip to Oaxaca, my incredible sex life, my special relationship to Jesus, etc., is borne with, heard out more or less politely, especially by women listening to men. But at length the true conversation continues around it, reconnecting unbroken, as water flows around a boulder. The conversation of the modest is what holds ordinary people together. It is the opposite of advertisement. It is communion.

"A LOVELY ART"
URSULA K. LE GUIN INTERVIEWED BY TERRY BISSON

What have you got against Amazon?

Nothing, really, except profound moral disapproval of their aims and methods, and a simple loathing of corporate greed.

Even though you occupy a pretty high perch in American Letters, you have never hesitated to describe yourself as a science fiction and fantasy author. Are you just being nice, or is there a plot behind this?

I am nice.

Also, the only means I have to stop ignorant snobs from behaving towards genre fiction with snobbish ignorance is to not reinforce their ignorance and snobbery by lying and saying that when I write SF it isn't SF, but to tell them more or less patiently for forty or fifty years that they are wrong to exclude SF and fantasy from literature, and proving my argument by writing well.

Your first Earthsea novel (1968) features a school for wizards. Some critics claim that you used your SF powers improperly to travel thirty years into the future and swipe the idea from J. K. Rowling. Do you deny this?

I plead the Fifth.

You once described yourself as a "fast and careless reader." I loved that! It reminded me of Dr. Johnson telling Boswell he rarely finished *a book. Do you still regard this as an advantage?*

Of course. It means I can get through shoddy books in no time, and can reread good books over and over …

One of the things I love about The Wild Girls *is its economy. You create a complex and strange world with a few swift strokes. William Gibson does this with art direction. How would you describe your technique?*

As improved by age and practice.

Should girls learn to sword fight?

I got in on my big brothers' fencing lessons when I was ten or twelve. It is a lovely art. I never planned to go out in the streets of Berkeley with my button foil looking for Bad Guys, however.

Your newest novel, Lavinia, *retells Virgil's* Aeneid *from a woman's point of view. Aeneas still plays the major role, though, and you seem rather fond of the dude. Do you like him better than Ulysses? Or Achilles?*

Ulysses is way too complicated to just like or dislike, but Achilles really turns me off. Sulky little egocentric squit. As if a lot of other guys on both sides didn't have to die young. I bet he went around with beard-stubble all over his face like all the sulky sullen half-baked heart-throb actors do.

Robert Louis Stevenson once said that our chronological age is like a scout, sent ahead of our "real" age which runs ten or fifteen years behind. What would you report back from your eightieth birthday?

I would like to be all cheer and bounce and lifewasneverbetter as old people—excuse me for bad language: older people—are expected to be. Unfortunately I find that at eighty I don't feel seventy let alone sixty-five. I feel eighty.

It isn't easy, but it's interesting.

You say you are not a "plotter." Do you start with an idea, or a character, or a situation? Or are they all the same thing?

Erm. Things come. People, landscapes, relationships among the people/landscapes. Situations begin to arise. I follow, watching and listening.

One criticism of the movie Avatar *was that there is no explanation for the convergent evolution. Is there one in your Ekumen books (I may have missed it)? Why not?*

Why not did you miss it? Why did you miss it not? Sir, I know not.

I provided a specious explanation of why everybody is more or less human: because everywhere local was settled by the Hainish. But that leaves out the indissoluble network of genetic relationship of *all* life on a planet. Such is the sleight of hand SF often has to play in order to get a story going. All we ask is the willing suspension of disbelief, which can and should return in full force when the novel is over.

You have generously mentored and promoted many emerging writers. Did anyone do the same for you?

I know everybody else remembers the early days of SFWA [Science Fiction Writers of America] as huge ego-competitions between X and Y and Z; but (maybe it was my practice at being a younger sister, or something?) I remember my early days in the SF world as being full of encouraging editors and fellow writers. Hey, what a neat bunch of people!

Seems to me it's easier to get published these days but harder to get noticed. How do you think you would fare starting out today?

If I hadn't connected with [literary agent] Virginia Kidd when I did, I might very well have had a much more constricted career and less visibility as a writer. Virginia was ready and able to sell anything I wrote—any length, any genre, to any editor.

I don't think it's easy to get published these days,

though. Not published so as it matters. Put stuff up on the Net, sure. Then what?

Have you ever been attacked by lions?

Three separate dogs have bitten me, many separate cats have bitten me, and recently my ankles underwent a terrifying siege by a bantam rooster at whom I had to kick dirt until he backed off and stood there all puffed up and shouting bad language like a Republican on Fox TV.

Who needs lions?

Many authors (including myself) have imitated your shape-shifting dream-altered world in The Lathe of Heaven. *Was this idea original to you or did you swipe it from someone else?*

A lot of stuff in *Lathe* is (obviously) influenced by and homage to Phil Dick. But the idea of dreams that alter reality seems to me a worldwide commonplace of magical thinking. Am I wrong? Did I make it up? Doctor, am I all right?

What's an ansible? Is it like a Kindle? Where can I get one?

Anarres.

You didn't seem too enthusiastic about the TV series based on your Earthsea *novels. Why not?*

It wasn't a series, and it wasn't Earthsea, and can I go have a drink now?

You once described the downtime between novels as like waiting patiently at the edge of the woods for a deer to walk by. Are you a bow hunter?

Of the mind.

"Travel is bad for fiction but good for poetry." Huh?

Just reporting my own experience as a writer.

I share your modest enthusiasm for Austen's Mansfield Park. *I didn't like the movie, though. Do you like any of the recent Jane movies?*

Oh, as movies, sure. Not as Austen. There is no way I can dislike Alan whatshisname with the voice like a cello.

What's your house like? Does your writing room have a view?

Nice, comfortable.

My study looks straight out at a volcano which blew off its top two thousand feet thirty years ago. I got to watch.

Perhaps your most famous and influential novel is The Left Hand of Darkness. *What's it about?*

People tell me what my books are about.

One problem writers have with utopias is that nothing bad can happen. You don't seem to have this problem. Is this a function of literary technique or philosophy?

Both. Places where nothing bad happens and nobody behaves badly are improbable, and unpromising for narrative.

You mentioned as your favorite repeated readings Dickens, Tolstoy, Austen, etc. Are there any Americans you go back to? Any SF or fantasy?

Let me off this question. I read too much.

What kind of car do you drive? (I ask this of everyone.)

Ha ha. I don't.

Charles is currently driving a Honda CR-V with about 120,000 on it. My favorite car we ever had was a red 1968 VW bus.

We all know better than to rate our contemporaries. But I would love to know your take on the late Walter M. Miller Jr., since he seemed to share your deep and radically humane conservatism.

He was a very, very good writer who I feel lucky to have read early on, so I could learn about the scope of SF from him.

The Ekumen and Earthsea series almost seem like bookends, one SF and one Fantasy. Where would you put Lavinia *on the shelf between?*

My writing is all over the map; bookends won't work. Even shelves won't work. *Lavinia* is what it is.

Lavinia *shows a great love for Rome, or at least pre-Roman virtues. That seems contrarian for a staunch progressive. Or is it?*

I am not a progressive. I think the idea of progress an invidious and generally harmful mistake. I am interested in change, which is an entirely different matter.

I like stiff, stuffy, earnest, serious, conscientious, responsible people, like Mr. Darcy and the Romans.

How's your Latin?

Mediocris.

Dragons are good in Earthsea. Or are they?

No. Nor bad. Other. Wild.

What have you got against Google?

Just its mistaken idea that it can ignore copyright and still do no harm.

In Always Coming Home *the future looks a lot like the past. What are the Kesh trying to tell us?*

What past does that future look like? I don't know anybody like the Kesh anywhere anywhen.

The countryside, of course, is the Napa Valley before (or after) agribusiness ruined it, but gee, we have to take our paradises where we find them.

The Dispossessed *is about an anarchist utopia, at least in part. So is* Always Coming Home. *Would you describe yourself as an anarchist (politically)?*

Politically, no; I vote, I'm a Democrat. But I find pacificist anarchist thought fascinating, stimulating, endlessly fruitful.

In your acknowledgements to Lavinia, *you praise your editor Mike Kandel. Is this the same Kandel who writes hilariously weird SF?*

He has translated Stanislaw Lem and others, marvelously. If he's written SF himself he's successfully hidden it from me. I wouldn't put it past him. Michael? What have I been missing?

I'm working on the cover copy for this book right now. Is it OK if I call your piece on modesty "the single greatest thing ever written on the subject"?

I think "the single finest, most perceptive, most gut-wrenchingly incandescent fucking piece of prose ever not written by somebody called Jonathan something" might be more precise.

Ezra Pound described poetry as "news that stays news." How do you see it? What poets do you read most often these days?

Lately I've been getting news again from old Robinson Jeffers. It isn't cheery but it's reliable.

In The Lathe of Heaven, *the first SF novel to take on (or even mention) global warming, the only big cities in Oregon are John Day and French Glen. Where the hell is French Glen?*

Did I spell it that way? It's one word: Frenchglen. It's in Harney County, in farthest southeast Oregon; pop. about twenty-five.

Do you ever get bad reviews? Was one ever helpful?

Yes. No.

This is my Jeopardy *item. The category is Mainstream Fiction. The answer is "One would hope." You provide the question.*

Erm?

One more, please. The category is Sitting Presidents. The answer is "One would hope not."

I'm really pretty good at Ghosts and Hangman.

What's your favorite gadget?

My MacBook Pro.

What's your writing discipline? Has it changed as you've gotten older? More successful?

I never had any discipline, I just really wanted to write when I wanted to write. So I can't say that it has gotten any more successful.

What's your favorite city and don't say Portland because it isn't really a city at all.

All right then, snob. Frenchglen.

My favorite writer (next to you, of course), R. A. Lafferty, once said that no writer has anything to say before age forty. He also once said that no writer has anything to say after forty. Do you agree?

I would never disagree with R. A. Lafferty.

In your pictures you seem to be laughing a lot. What's so funny?

Cf. A. E. Housman: "Mithridates, he died old."

Will you sign my baseball? It's for my daughter.

If you will sign my fencing foil.

BIBLIOGRAPHY

Major works only, principal U.S. editions only

NOVELS

Novels of the Ekumen:
The Telling. Harcourt, 2000; Gollancz, 2001.
The Word for World Is Forest. Putnam, 1976; Berkley,
    1976.
The Dispossessed: An Ambiguous Utopia. Harper & Row,
    1974; Avon, 1975.
The Left Hand of Darkness. Walker, 1969; Ace, 1969;
    Harper & Row, 1980.
City of Illusions. Ace, 1967; Harper & Row, 1978.
Planet of Exile. Ace, 1966; Harper & Row, 1978.
Rocannon's World. Ace, 1966; Harper & Row, 1977.
(These three reissued in one volume as *Worlds of Exile and
    Illusion*, Tor, 1998.)

The Books of Earthsea:
The Other Wind. Harcourt, 2001.
Tales from Earthsea. Harcourt, 2001.
Tehanu. Atheneum,1990; Bantam, 1991.
The Farthest Shore. Atheneum, 1972; Bantam, 1975.
The Tombs of Atuan. Atheneum, 1970; Bantam, 1975.
A Wizard of Earthsea. Parnassus/Houghton Mifflin, 1968; Ace,
      1970; Atheneum, 1991.

The Annals of the Western Shore:
Gifts. Harcourt, 2004.
Voices. Harcourt, 2006.
Powers. Harcourt, 2007.

Other Novels:
Lavinia. Harcourt, 2008.
Always Coming Home. Harper & Row, 1985; Bantam,
      1987; U.C. Press, 2000.
The Eye of the Heron. Harper & Row, 1983; Bantam,
      1983.
The Beginning Place. Harper & Row, 1980; Bantam,1981.
Malafrena. Putnam, 1979; Berkely, 1980.
Very Far Away from Anywhere Else. Atheneum, 1976;
      Bantam, 1978.
The Lathe of Heaven. Scribners, 1971; Avon, 1972;
      Scribners, 2008.

STORY COLLECTIONS

Changing Planes. Harcourt, 2003; Mythopoeic Society
      Award nomination, 2004.

The Birthday of the World. HarperCollins, 2002.

Unlocking the Air. Harper Collins, 1996.

Four Ways to Forgiveness. Harper Prism, 1995; pb, 1996.

A Fisherman of the Inland Sea. Harper Prism,1994; pb, 1995.

Searoad. HarperCollins, 1991; pb, 1992.

Buffalo Gals. Capra,1987; NAL 1988.

The Compass Rose. Underwood-Miller, 1982; Harper & Row, 1982; Bantam, 1983.

Orsinian Tales. Harper & Row, 1976; Bantam, 1977.

The Wind's Twelve Quarters. Harper & Row, 1975; Bantam, 1976.

POETRY

Incredible Good Fortune. Shambhala, 2006.

Sixty Odd. Shambhala, 1999.

Going out with Peacocks. HarperCollins, 1994.

Blue Moon over Thurman Street (with Roger Dorband). NewSage, 1993.

Wild Oats and Fireweed. Harper & Row, 1988.

Hard Words. Harper & Row, 1981.

Wild Angels. Capra, 1974.

TRANSLATIONS

Selected Poems of Gabriela Mistral. University of New Mexico Press, 2003.

Kalpa Imperial. (Angelica Gorodischer). Small Beer Press, 2003.

The Twins, The Dream/Las Gemelas, El Sueno (with Diana
    Bellessi). Arte Publico Press, 1997; Ed. Norma,
    1998.
*Lao Tzu: Tao Te Ching: Book About The Way and the Power
    of the Way.* Shambhala, 1997, 2009. New edition
    includes two CDs. Music by Todd Barton.

CRITICISM

Cheek by Jowl. Aqueduct, 2009.
The Wave in the Mind. Shambhala, 2004.
Steering the Craft. Eighth Mountain, 1998.
The Language of the Night (revised ed.). HarperCollins,
    1992.
Dancing at the Edge of the World. Grove, 1989.

BOOKS FOR CHILDREN

The Catwings Books (illus. S. D. Schindler), 1988–1999:
Catwings. Orchard.
Catwings Return. Orchard.
Wonderful Alexander and the Catwings. Orchard.
Jane on Her Own. Orchard.

Other Books for Children:
Cat Dreams (illus. S. D. Schindler). Scholastic, 2010.
Tom Mouse (illus. J. Downing). Roaring Brook, 2002.
A Ride on the Red Mare's Back (illus. J. Downing).
    Orchard, 1992. pb, 1993.
Fish Soup (illus. P. Wynne). Atheneum, 1992.

Fire and Stone (illus. L. Marshall). Atheneum, 1989.
A Visit from Dr. Katz (illus. A. Barrow). Atheneum, 1988.
Solomon Leviathan (illus. A. Austin). Philomel, 1988.
Cobbler's Rune (illus. A. Austin). Cheap Street, 1983.
Leese Webster (illus. James Brunsman). Atheneum, 1979.

ANTHOLOGIES EDITED

The Norton Book of Science Fiction (with Brian Attebery and Karen Fowler). Norton, 1993.
Edges. With Virginia Kidd. Pocket Books, 1980.
Interfaces. With Virginia Kidd. Grosset & Dunlap/Ace, 1980.
Nebula Award Stories XI. Harper & Row, 1977.

SCREENPLAY IN BOOK FORMAT

King Dog. Capra, 1985.

CHAPBOOKS

The Art of Bunditsu. Ygor & Buntho Make Books Press, 1993.
Findings. Ox Head, 1992.
No Boats. Ygor & Buntho Make Books Press, 1992.
A Winter Solstice Ritual for the Pacific Northwest (with Vonda N. McIntyre). Ygor & Buntho Make Books Press, 1991.
In the Red Zone (with Henk Pander). Lord John, 1983.

Tillai and Tylissos (with Theodora Kroeber). Red Bull, 1979.

Walking in Cornwall. n.p. 1976. Reprinted, Crescent Moon, 2008.

The Water Is Wide. Pendragon Press, 1976.

ABOUT THE AUTHOR

URSULA K. LE GUIN WAS BORN A Kroeber in Berkeley, California. Her mother was a psychologist and writer; her father was the chair of University of California–Berkeley's Anthropology Department. "My father studied real cultures and I make them up," she once said. "In a way, the same thing."

After attending Radcliffe and Columbia (MA, French Literature) she studied in Paris on a Fulbright scholarship, where she met and married historian Charles Le Guin.

They returned to the United States on the *Queen Mary*. After a few years of teaching, she began to write fiction.

Since her first published stories in the 1960s, Le Guin has been a major force in science fiction and fantasy. *The Left Hand of Darkness*, exploring a culture without gender, placed her at the center of the political/feminist/literary movement elevating SF to a new maturity. Her Earthsea fantasies and her somber SF novels of the interstellar Ekumen have influenced, illuminated, and entertained readers worldwide for almost fifty years. She has also written poetry and essays on social and literary themes.

Among the many honors her work has received are a National Book Award, five Hugo Awards, five Nebula Awards, SFWA's Grand Master, the Kafka Award, a Pushcart Prize, the Howard Vursell Award of the American Academy of Arts and Letters and the PEN/Malamud Award.

Critic Harold Bloom includes her on his list of classic American authors. Novelist Margaret Atwood is more specific and less reserved: "Within the frequently messy sandbox of sci-fi fantasy, some of the most accomplished and suggestive intellectual play of the last century has taken place. Which brings us to Ursula K. Le Guin . . ."

She lives in Portland, Oregon.

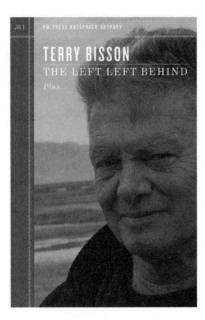

PM PRESS
OUTSPOKEN AUTHORS

The Left Left Behind
Terry Bisson
978-1-60486-086-3
$12

Hugo and Nebula award-winner Terry Bisson is best known for his short stories, which range from the southern sweetness of "Bears Discover Fire" to the alienated aliens of "They're Made out of Meat." He is also a 1960s New Left vet with a history of activism and an intact (if battered) radical ideology.

The *Left Behind* novels (about the so-called "Rapture" in which all the born-agains ascend straight to heaven) are among the bestselling Christian books in the U.S., describing in lurid detail the adventures of those "left behind" to battle the Anti-Christ. Put Bisson and the Born-Agains together, and what do you get? *The Left Left Behind*—a sardonic, merciless, tasteless, take-no-prisoners satire of the entire apocalyptic enterprise that spares no one-predatory preachers, goth lingerie, Pacifica radio, Indian casinos, gangsta rap, and even "art cars" at Burning Man.

Plus: "Special Relativity," a one-act drama that answers the question: When Albert Einstein, Paul Robeson, J. Edgar Hoover are raised from the dead at an anti-Bush rally, which one wears the dress? As with all Outspoken Author books, there is a deep interview and autobiography: at length, in-depth, no-holds-barred, and all-bets-off: an extended tour though the mind and work, the history and politics of our Outspoken Author. Surprises are promised.

PM PRESS
OUTSPOKEN AUTHORS

The Lucky Strike
Kim Stanley Robinson
978-1-60486-085-6
$12

Combining dazzling speculation with a profoundly humanist vision, Kim Stanley Robinson is known as not only the most literary but also the most progressive (read "radical") of today's top-rank SF authors. His bestselling Mars Trilogy tells the epic story of the future colonization of the red planet, and the revolution that inevitably follows. His latest novel, *Galileo's Dream*, is a stunning combination of historical drama and far-flung space opera, in which the ten dimensions of the universe itself are rewoven to ensnare history's most notorious torturers.

The Lucky Strike, the classic and controversial story Robinson has chosen for PM's new Outspoken Authors series, begins on a lonely Pacific island, where a crew of untested men are about to take off in an untried aircraft with a deadly payload that will change our world forever. Until something goes wonderfully wrong.

Plus: *A Sensitive Dependence on Initial Conditions*, in which Robinson dramatically deconstructs "alternate history" to explore what might have been if things had gone differently over Hiroshima that day.

As with all Outspoken Author books, there is a deep interview and autobiography: at length, in-depth, no-holds-barred and all-bets-off: an extended tour though the mind and work, the history and politics of our Outspoken Author. Surprises are promised.

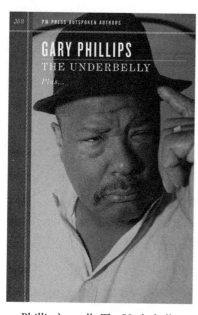

PM PRESS
OUTSPOKEN AUTHORS

The Underbelly
Gary Phillips
978-1-60486-206-5
$12

The explosion of wealth and development in downtown L.A. is a thing of wonder. But regardless of how big and shiny our buildings get, we should not forget the ones this wealth and development has overlooked and pushed out. This is the context for Phillips' novella The Underbelly, as a semi-homeless Vietnam vet named Magrady searches for a wheelchair-bound friend gone missing from Skid Row--a friend who might be working a dangerous scheme against major players. Magrady's journey is a solo sortie where the flashback-prone protagonist must deal with the impact of gentrification; take-no-prisoners community organizers; an unflinching cop from his past in Vietnam; an elderly sexpot out for his bones; a lusted-after magical skull; chronic-lovin' knuckleheads; and the perils of chili cheese fries at midnight. Combining action, humor and a street level gritty POV, *The Underbelly* is illustrated with photos and drawings.

Plus: a rollicking interview wherein Phillips riffs on Ghetto Lit, politics, noir and the proletariat, the good negroes and bad knee-grows of pop culture, Redd Foxx and Lord Buckley, and wrestles with the future of books in the age of want.

Praise:
"...honesty, distinctive characters, absurdity and good writing—are here in Phillips's work." —*The Washington Post*

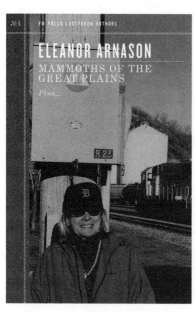

PM PRESS
OUTSPOKEN AUTHORS

Mammoths of the Great Plains
Eleanor Arnason
978-1-60486-075-7
$12

When President Thomas Jefferson sent Lewis and Clark to explore the West, he told them to look especially for mammoths. Jefferson had seen bones and tusks of the great beasts in Virginia, and he suspected—he hoped!—that they might still roam the Great Plains. In Eleanor Arnason's imaginative alternate history, they do: shaggy herds thunder over the grasslands, living symbols of the oncoming struggle between the Native peoples and the European invaders. And in an unforgettable saga that soars from the badlands of the Dakotas to the icy wastes of Siberia, from the Russian Revolution to the AIM protests of the 1960s, Arnason tells of a modern woman's struggle to use the weapons of DNA science to fulfill the ancient promises of her Lakota heritage.

Plus: "Writing SF During World War III," and an Outspoken Interview that takes you straight into the heart and mind of one of today's edgiest and most uncompromising speculative authors.

Praise:
"Eleanor Arnason nudges both human and natural history around so gently in this tale that you hardly know you're not in the world-as-we-know-it until you're quite at home in a North Dakota where you've never been before, listening to your grandmother tell you the world."   —Ursula K. Le Guin

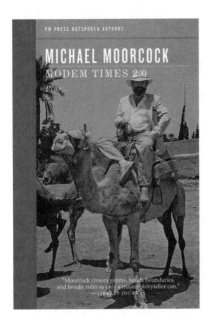

PM PRESS OUTSPOKEN AUTHORS

Modem Times 2.0
Michael Moorcock
978-1-60486-308-6
$12

As the editor of London's revolutionary *New Worlds* magazine in the swinging sixties, Michael Moorcock has been credited with virtually inventing modern Science Fiction: publishing such figures as Norman Spinrad, Samuel R. Delany, Brian Aldiss and J.G. Ballard.

Moorcock's own literary accomplishments include his classic "Mother London," a romp through urban history conducted by psychic outsiders; his comic Pyat quartet, in which a Jewish antisemite examines the roots of the Nazi Holocaust; Behold The Man, the tale of a time tourist who fills in for Christ on the cross; and of course the eternal hero Elric, swordswinger, hellbringer and bestseller.

And now Moorcock's most audacious creation, Jerry Cornelius—assassin, rock star, chronospy and maybe-Messiah—is back in *Modem Times 2.0*, a time twisting odyssey that connects 60s London with post-Obama America, with stops in Palm Springs and Guantanamo. *Modem Times 2.0* is Moorcock at his most outrageously readable—a masterful mix of erudition and subversion.

Plus: a non-fiction romp in the spirit of Swift and Orwell, Fields of Folly; and an Outspoken Interview with literature's authentic Lord of Misrule.

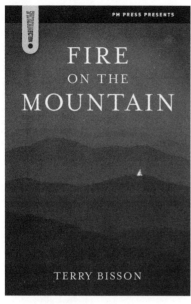

It's 1959 in socialist Virginia. The Deep South is an independent Black nation called Nova Africa. The second Mars expedition is about to touch down on the red planet. And a pregnant scientist is climbing the Blue Ridge in search of her great-great grandfather, a teenage slave who fought with John Brown and Harriet Tubman's guerrilla army.

Long unavailable in the U.S., published in France as *Nova Africa*, *Fire on the Mountain* is the story of what might have happened if John Brown's raid on Harper's Ferry had succeeded—and the Civil War had been started not by the slave owners but the abolitionists.

Praise:
"History revisioned, turned inside out ... Bisson's wild and wonderful imagination has taken some strange turns to arrive at such a destination."
—Madison Smartt Bell, Anisfield-Wolf Award winner and author of *Devil's Dream*.

"You don't forget Bisson's characters, even well after you've finished his books. His Fire on the Mountain does for the Civil War what Philip K. Dick's *The Man in the High Castle* did for World War Two."
—George Alec Effinger, winner of the Hugo and Nebula awards for *Shrödinger's Kitten*, and author of the *Marîd Audran* trilogy.

PM PRESS
FOUND IN TRANSLATION

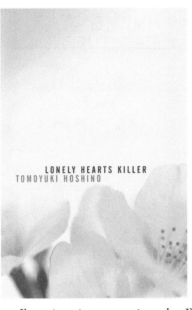

Lonely Hearts Killer
Tomoyuki Hoshino
Translated by Adrienne
Carey Hurley
978-1-60486-084-9
$15.95

"I don't want to go so far as to say such-and-such was the deciding factor. Only that it's too late now. From this point onward, we have no choice but to rebuild our relationships anew. For that to happen ... I've written it so many times that I'm not rehashing it yet again."

What happens when a popular and young emperor suddenly dies and the only person available to succeed him is his sister? How can people in an island country survive as climate change and martial law are eroding more and more opportunities for local sustainability and mutual aid? Where can people turn when the wildly distorted stories told on the nightly news are about them? And what can be done to challenge the rise of a new authoritarian political leadership at a time when the general public is obsessed with fears related to personal and national "security"? These and other provocative questions provide the backdrop for this powerhouse novel about young adults embroiled in what appear to be more private matters – friendships, sex, a love suicide, and struggles to cope with grief and work. *Lonely Hearts Killer* compels readers to examine the relationship between state violence and interpersonal brutality while pointing toward ways out of the escalating terror. PM Press is proud to bring you this first English translation of a full-length novel by the award-winning Japanese author Tomoyuki Hoshino.

FRIENDS OF

These are indisputably momentous times—the financial system is melting down globally and the Empire is stumbling. Now more than ever there is a vital need for radical ideas.

In the three years since its founding—and on a mere shoestring—PM Press has risen to the formidable challenge of publishing and distributing knowledge and entertainment for the struggles ahead. With over 100 releases to date, we have published an impressive and stimulating array of literature, art, music, politics, and culture. Using every available medium, we've succeeded in connecting those hungry for ideas and information to those putting them into practice.

Friends of PM allows you to directly help impact, amplify, and revitalize the discourse and actions of radical writers, filmmakers, and artists. It provides us with a stable foundation from which we can build upon our early successes and provides a much-needed subsidy for the materials that can't necessarily pay their own way. You can help make that happen – and receive every new title automatically delivered to your door once a month – by joining as a Friend of PM Press. And, we'll throw in a free T-Shirt when you sign up.

Here are your options:

• $25 a month: Get all books and pamphlets plus 50% discount on all webstore purchases.

• $25 a month: Get all CDs and DVDs plus 50% discount on all webstore purchases.

• $40 a month: Get all PM Press releases plus 50% discount on all webstore purchases

• $100 a month: Sustainer. - Everything plus PM merchandise, free downloads, and 50% discount on all webstore purchases.

For those who can't afford $25 or more a month, we're introducing Sustainer Rates at $15, $10 and $5. Sustainers get a free PM Press t-shirt and a 50% discount on all purchases from our website.

Just go to **WWW.PMPRESS.ORG** to sign up. Your Visa or Mastercard will be billed once a month, until you tell us to stop. Or until our efforts succeed in bringing the revolution around. Or the financial meltdown of Capital makes plastic redundant. Whichever comes first.

PM PRESS was founded at the end of 2007 by a small collection of folks with decades of publishing, media, and organizing experience. PM Press co-conspirators have published and distributed hundreds of books, pamphlets, CDs, and DVDs. Members of PM have founded enduring book fairs, spearheaded victorious tenant organizing campaigns, and worked closely with bookstores, academic conferences, and even rock bands to deliver political and challenging ideas to all walks of life. We're old enough to know what we're doing and young enough to know what's at stake.

We seek to create radical and stimulating fiction and non-fiction books, pamphlets, t-shirts, visual and audio materials to entertain, educate and inspire you. We aim to distribute these through every available channel with every available technology—whether that means you are seeing anarchist classics at our bookfair stalls; reading our latest vegan cookbook at the café; downloading geeky fiction e-books; or digging new music and timely videos from our website.

PM Press is always on the lookout for talented and skilled volunteers, artists, activists and writers to work with. If you have a great idea for a project or can contribute in some way, please get in touch.

PM PRESS
PO Box 23912
Oakland CA 94623
510-658-3906
www.pmpress.org